O₂

A NOVEL BY

S DAIGNAULT

EARTH'S LAST BREATH

Dedication

*To my sisters who are my best friends, and
to my best friends who are my sisters*

CHAPTER
ONE

• •

December 5, 2039

Beijing, China

Zhang Wei rode his bicycle, expertly navigating around the vehicles and people congesting the streets of the city. It was seven a.m. and the air quality reports were worse than yesterday. Beijing had the poorest quality in the world. He wondered if it would ever change. He coughed into his mask contemplating the striking difference of when he was a young boy.

He moved his hand to readjust the elastic behind his ear and caught himself swerving before slamming into a passenger exiting a parked car. The near miss shook his focus back to the street and his job at the treatment plant. Dreary and hard work but worth it. Wei and his wife wanted to make a better life for their children. His oldest son's acceptance into the university eased his mind – oh, the joy he had felt last night! His son announced he wanted to study anthropology. Wei wanted him to study environmental sciences. But who was he to be picky? His position at the treatment plant was the highest level he would ever achieve. His son would break out and be someone special. He pictured how everyone in the family of brothers, sisters, aunts, and uncles would be so proud.

His heart raced, and his breath became hard to catch. Just excited about the news he thought. He started coughing again – that annoying cough that never went away. His bicycle, as if it had a will of its own, veered to the left and slid out from underneath his body. It was a slow-motion action that played out in his head. What was happening to him? The ground came up hard beneath him.

People crowded around his body as he stared up into their faces and beyond to a clouded, polluted sky, unable to breathe.

Siberia, Russia

Olga had seen too many winters in her life. She grunted and then laughed into her empty cold kitchen. In Siberia there was only winter. She was ready to leave this earth. At 106 years old she felt content. She had lived a good life. Children, grandchildren, great grandchildren, and even one great-great.

This morning her bones ached more than usual. But chores waited and she pushed herself out of the chair and went outside to fill a bucket of water for the barn animals. It was a short walk to the barn from the house she had lived in for 80 years with her husband. *Was it already over twenty years since he passed?* She struggled with the bucket, dragging it across the snow and wished she had one of her grandchildren to help. The air today seemed particularly cold against her lungs, as if it was freezing them from the inside. Just a few more steps and she'd be sheltered in the barn. The animals' body heat would make the inside welcoming. I'll catch my breath when I get inside, was her last thought before she collapsed in a mound of snow.

Tanzania, East Africa

Imani ran as fast as he could. He had practiced running every day this past week. All his friends were participating in the local village's race to support new computers for the classrooms. The race was sponsored by some rich, fancy man from London. He had no idea who the man was, all he knew was a video of the race would be uploaded to major communications companies around the world. He wanted to win. There were older boys running, even one four years older, who turned fifteen last month. This only made him more committed. They wouldn't stop him and neither would his asthma. His mama gave him medicine every day. Mama worried about him all the time, never letting him play like the other boys.

But this past week after he heard about the race he had snuck out before she woke and practiced. He would show her and the whole village how strong he was. People would notice him for his running, not his asthma. He approached a bend in the dirt road where the shade of the acacia tree offered an inviting place to rest. Every morning during his practices he had stopped to enjoy a moment to sit under the branches. Today he pushed himself without stopping. He saw the outline of the village against the sky and a terrifying feeling gripped his chest. His legs buckled and crumpled into the red dirt.

Chicago, Illinois

The eighty-fifth floor of the high rise offered an unparalleled view of Lake Michigan. Unlike many other major cities situated on a coastline, Chicago was not completely overcome by rising water levels. Frank sat alone in the corner conference room unable to think clearly. This presentation had been his last effort to save the family-owned company, a company started by his great-grandfather. This was the last place to get the capital necessary to save it from bankruptcy, and he had failed. They didn't even give him the full hour to present his carefully crafted plan. The president of the bank stood up, shook his hand, and said, "We cannot entertain your proposal at this time." Everyone followed like ducks in a row. This was the end of his business not to mention his personal life. His wife had left weeks ago taking their son and daughter to her mother's place in Iowa. The house would foreclose in the next month and old friends were already dropping from sight. Hell, he wasn't even fifty yet. He sat there in the conference room. He would never make it out of this mess.

The administrative assistant cracked open the door and peeked in. "Sir, you'll have to leave now. The room is scheduled for another meeting in ten minutes." Frank jumped up from his chair. His head spun making him lean a hand on the mahogany conference table. He gasped for air but couldn't find enough of it.

CHAPTER
TWO

• •

One week earlier

Stanford, CA

"**C**arbon dioxide emissions are no longer the threat they once were in the early 2000's. We can now mitigate the risk of greenhouse gases impacting our environment across the globe." Dr Sydney Davis gazed out at the full auditorium, wrapping up her one-hour presentation. She motioned to the last slide on the large screen at her back, "As I have pointed out, the future issue will be a slow and steady depletion of oxygen. That is why the O_2 levels are now on the Institute's top earth-concerns list." With that final thought she let go of the lectern. She shook her left hand which had begun to tingle from her grip on the wooden structure.

A voice from the audience broke the silence, "What do you say about all this Dr. Davis?" Sydney recognized the voice as the president of Stanford University and their major funding benefactor, Dr. Harold Sworkin. The hall got quiet and she could feel the bodies in the room shift toward her right. Her stomach tightened. The question wasn't directed at her.

The large screen behind her dimmed and the lights came up as the woman on stage who had been sitting on the side stood up and moved forward with measured steps stopping directly in front of the lectern. She took another beat to gaze across the hall. All eyes were on her, waiting. "It's not what I say but what the facts dictate, Harry." Her mother never let an opportunity slip by for playing out her role as the most well-known and respected research-physician in the world. Would she ever get used to being in her mother's shadow?

A CEO from one of the large pharmas called out. "But have you seen any real impact yet? Even a tiny change in oxygen levels would start causing physiological changes. Are we seeing some of these? In people?"

As soon as he finished someone else pitched another question toward the stage, "Your Institute is responsible for maintaining balance on this planet. Not letting anything catastrophic happen. Isn't your motto 'Protect and Respect'? What are you doing about this?" It was obvious the audience was getting agitated. Hands raised across the auditorium.

"One at a time." Dr. Ann Davis straightened her spine extending to her intimidating height of 5'11". "We are doing something. That's what this presentation was about. We are informing you."

Sydney swung around the lectern and stood side by side with her mother. She knew they made a powerful presence. Both tall, both athletic and, annoyingly, most people took her mother for her sister. She finally found her voice, "We are far from disaster. This is a highly predictive model that estimated a possible depletion of oxygen over several hundreds of years. The Earth Institute is bound by ethical standards and its directive is to inform all heads of state, top business leaders and education institutions of findings that could impact the globe. Even when that impact is years into the future. This presentation is to give you direction for research and development within each of your organizations. We all have seen and know that even a hundred years is a drop in the bucket if we are to combat a crisis endangering the earth."

In the presentation, Sydney had informed the audience of fifty business and international leaders that the current oxygen rate was 20.6%. The atmosphere's normal rate was 20.9%. Maintaining the balance of oxygen is critical to earth's atmosphere. Not many people understood the delicate balance and what a tiny percentage change would mean. The scientists at the Institute had a hypothesis that accounted for the current 0.3% drop – the decreasing oxygen was caused by increasing microbial activity in the northern hemisphere. But the Institute didn't know the root cause. They were working on it but with no firm conclusion. She purposefully held back that information. However, the pharma CEO had alluded to the other part of the research that she didn't mention. If the oxygen rate dropped below 20.0%, the change would drastically impact all life on the planet. She shuddered. Then relaxed her shoulders telling herself it would never get that far. A 1% drop was a significant jump in percentage and, microbial activity would never make an impact of such magnitude. Anyway, they would stop whatever this was before then.

Dr. Ann Davis waved her hand back and forth dismissing the questions. "We will be providing updates on the levels on a quarterly basis along with additional research on the subject. I'm needed somewhere else right now." Without looking back, she turned and walked off stage. She was so good at leaving. Probably embedded in her DNA.

Sydney took a step forward and addressed the crowd, "I want to thank you for being here despite your busy schedules. I will answer all questions. And please, one at a time."

The session was exhausting but necessary. She stood on her feet, on that stage, answering questions for over an hour. At one point she succumbed to a fit of coughing from speaking so much. These were people who had to understand all issues threatening the earth and be able to make decisions regarding the future of the planet. They were the ones with the power. Her job was to inform, theirs was to enact change. She would make sure every person walked out of the hall knowing the vital importance of what she told them.

She took her time walking back to her office at the Institute. The headquarters were housed in a separate building within the compound of Stanford University's campus. She removed her light-wool jacket and hooked it on a finger swinging it around her back. Her linen t-shirt felt cool against her skin as the breeze filtered through. She allowed her mind to wander and take in the crispness of the November morning. She hadn't had a chance to run her usual five miles. Her legs wanted to move, to take off on one of the beautiful canyon trails. But her jeans wouldn't allow it. She followed the familiar winding path across the campus. She passed through the front entrance of the unobtrusive building where a granite stone announced, 'Earth Institute for Health and Welfare – Protect and Respect'. Her mother's name was etched in smaller letters underneath, 'Dr. Ann Davis, Founder, 2029'.

As soon as she got to her office, she peeled an orange sticky note from the laptop. Above the machine on the wall were more sticky notes in her handwriting. Notes for her doctors' appointments that kept getting cancelled and rescheduled. Notes from old friends from college. Reunion? No way. Her days were jam packed with meetings, travel to research labs, managing her teams across the country. Did she ever have a normal life? She kept the notes to remind her that there was more out there. Someday, perhaps. A framed picture captured the moment her doctoral hood was placed over her head. The only nod to her past life. Her life before she started working at the Institute.

She glanced back at the orange sticky note but before she could read it, a short man with wisps of dark hair barely covering a bald head rushed in. "Finally, you're back. Did you read my note?"

She half-smiled at him and tilted her head. "Good morning, Dar. How are you today? By the way, I'm good." She held a finger up, "well, maybe a little tired after answering questions for over an hour this morning." Sydney liked him. He was about five years older and unfortunately never quite appreciated her sarcasm.

Darweshi furrowed his brows. His clothes looked like they needed a good wash. He was thirtyeight and never married. Today he wore the blue-collared shirt with the Earth Institute logo he received when he first arrived. "I'm good, fine . . . well . . . maybe not good or fine, but okay."

Sydney crumbled the note he had left, figuring he'd tell her about it and settled into her chair. He'd been at the Institute for eight years, almost as long as she'd been. Over those years her relationship with Dar settled somewhere between a friend and co-worker.

"Your fellowship candidate has arrived and he's been waiting in the conference room for about forty-five minutes."

"Oh no!" She shot up and uncrumpled the note, "I forgot all about him. Why didn't you say so right away?" She moved around him toward the door. "What's his name? Young?"

"Li Yun." Darweshi said to her back.

Sydney raced down the hall toward the large conference room. She pushed open the door, "I'm sorry to keep you waiting. Lots going on here today." She sat down at the head of the early 1900's antique, scarred mahogany table next to the young man. Much of the furniture at the Institute was to her mother's taste. She hated it. Old, dark, and uncomfortable. Dark eyes followed her. His jet-black hair was chin-length and partially hid his face. He had a small dragon tattoo on his wrist. She knew from his records that he was eighteen. She tried to look beyond the youthful appearance and caught a glimpse of a deep, serious young man. It was as if he carried the weight of every problem behind those dark eyes. She smiled. He didn't smile back.

His curriculum vitae revealed basic information. He had come to the United States at thirteen from mainland China after being accepted at several prestigious universities. That didn't surprise her since she herself had attended college in Boston at fifteen. He received his doctorate five years later in evolutionary botany from Stanford and had applied to the Institute's fellowship program. He had been accepted because of his research on the evolutionary links between earth's biosphere and geology.

"Mr. Yun . . . sorry, I mean Mr. Li, I'm very happy to meet you. We're excited to have you in our fellowship program. With everything we do here I believe your expertise will be the perfect complement."

"Please call me Yun." He kept his eyes on her face. He stretched out his legs under the table and hit her foot. Long legs. She guessed he was probably close to her height.

She moved her foot, "Great. Well, Yun, I'm sure you have looked up the background on the Institute when you applied. But let me go over a few things." Sydney took a second, thinking he might say something or nod his head for her to continue. After another second without any acknowledgement, she folded her hands and leaned back in the chair. "I'll start at the beginning. It'll help give you the full picture of who we are. The Institute for Earth, Health and Welfare was founded by Dr. Ann Davis in 2029. After receiving her doctorate in medicine from Harvard and residency at Mass General, she dedicated her life to research rather than a practice. The

Institute's mission is to provide information backed by extensive research, conducted at this location, for leaders of the world to enact changes and thereby ensure the earth will flourish for generations to come. Dr. Ann Davis is the linchpin with her connections across the globe and the prestige she gained over the years as the most sought-after research physician for her ground-breaking work during the 2020's linking the health of the earth to the health of the individual. No one had ever proven that the mental and physical state of a person are inexorably connected through the brain to the earth. To every living organism."

"We, in the East, always believed this concept. The earth and man are one."

Sydney straightened up in her chair. "You're right, of course." She said, "However, what my mother did was prove the connection with physical evidence and experimentation." While her mother was a supporter of all that the Institute embraced, and her initial research that made her famous did much to merge the borders between man and his environment, her need for power and control was at the heart of any environmental concern. It was at the heart of everything she did.

"Dr. Ann Davis is your mother?" He was going to find out anyway. If people only knew how unmotherly she was.

"Yes. She recruited me . . ." Sydney pushed some papers around. Recruited was an interesting word. It was more like summoned. ". . . right after I received my doctorate. I've been with her; I mean here at the Institute for almost ten years. I am the head geophysicist and you'll report to me."

Yun sat back in his chair and seemed to consider something important. A moment later he pulled forward and locked eyes with her, "I'm anxious to get started."

Back in her office she went through the latest reports on oxygen levels. Holding at 20.6. Not that she expected any change from what she read that morning. She'd check again in another hour. She was glad to have Yun. He warmed up a bit during the orientation. He promised to be an excellent addition to her team. She knew when she had read his doctoral thesis on shifting patterns of plants over millions of years on the earth's geological environment that he would close a critical gap in the Institute's expertise. Sydney considered it her intuition for seeing today what would be important in the future, a talent. Isn't that why her mother wanted her there? Certainly not because she wanted to be close to her only child. She brushed her fingers through her cropped hair and then massaged her neck. She could feel the bristly edges at the nape.

Bianca, her hairdresser had asked about this. "Are you sure you want it this short? You should be showing off those beautiful blonde locks."

"Yes, well. I've got too much going on to be concerned about my hair." She decided she liked it this short. Made her feel less weighted-down.

Twilight came quickly at this time of year. She stopped typing and slid her chair closer to the window. The sky was like an indigo abstract painting with wisps of fog revealing indistinct flickers of light. Sydney loved art especially abstract and whenever her schedule allowed, she wandered through the local galleries. In her office across from her desk, she had splurged on a lithograph by Miro.

She loved both the chaos and the formality of the piece. That's what excited her about abstract — it could be both. The piece reminded her of the canyons that she tackled on her runs. Sydney let her mind wander. She drifted and saw herself holding onto someone who guided her through a mountainous path. That someone had no face. But it was a good feeling; safe, comfortable. She shook her head and blinked to focus on her computer. She didn't know how long she'd been staring out her office window.

"Sydney . . . Sydney!"

She spun in her chair.

"What's wrong with you?"

"Nothing. Nothing is wrong, Mother."

"Daydreaming again? You need to get control over whatever it is you were doing."

How could her mother ever understand daydreaming? Sometimes she thought she wasn't even human. "It helps me think. Believe it or not it's proven to increase the link between creative and logical processes in the brain." A scientific explanation was the only argument accepted. Her mother opposed any information that was not backed by cold, hard facts.

"Whatever." Dr. Davis did a hand-wave dismissal. "Have you gotten Li Yun established in his office? Given him an orientation? Assigned some immediate tasks? You need to have him looking at geological changes in the northern hemisphere as soon as possible."

Sydney gritted her teeth. Why did no one else in the world see the real Dr. Davis. "Yes, yes and yes."

"Good. I'm flying out to meet with the Eastern Coalition tomorrow morning. When I get back, I'll want an update on the O_2 levels and a plan regarding the root cause analysis for the microbial activity."

"No problem. Have a good flight." Sydney turned back to her computer.

Dr. Davis walked toward the door then stopped short and turned back. "And please have that Darweshi fellow stop making those god-awful soups in the lunch area. The smell is an assault. What does he do here, again?"

"Our climatologist. A top and well-known expert in his field." She spoke into empty space. Her mother hadn't waited for a reply.

CHAPTER
THREE

Sydney, engrossed in hearing her feet hitting the hard dirt of the canyon path, didn't notice that she had turned up toward the cliffs. Since presentation, the four days ago her mind couldn't stop analyzing scenarios of possible causes for the reduced oxygen. The rhythm of her body broke as she tripped over an obstacle, landing face first in the dirt. Sydney's scream reverberated into the canyon void. It was a woman's body. Motionless, it teetered at the cliff edge. Sydney paralyzed with an age-old fear froze staring into the deep blue sky beyond the hills overlooking the South Bay. She managed to push her body up but couldn't find the strength to do much else. The familiar dizziness overcame her senses. She attempted to control her breath as she played back all those meditation sessions she had watched online. It was no use. She gulped air in between her yells as two runners from the trail below raced up the side following her voice. A man and woman scanned the scene and quickly knelt beside the unconscious woman. Sydney backed away, step by step, until she felt the bark of a pine tree pinch through her sweatshirt and used it as a guide sliding her body to the ground. Within seconds, her acrophobia had kicked into full gear. Through her daze she heard the man connect with emergency assistance giving them directions.

"I hear there was an incident on the South Bay trail this morning." Darweshi popped a piece of buttered toast into his mouth as he stepped into her office.

Sydney picked her head up from the screen, her eyes blurred from strain. She'd been reviewing the morning update for her mother who returned yesterday. Dr. Davis expected it in five minutes. Darweshi's habit of starting a conversation without any preamble and assuming she was available to talk to him whenever, never bothered her, but today she was not in the mood. "Yes, a woman collapsed in front of me on my morning run." She waved her hand back and forth. Then stopped in mid-wave. Geez, did she just do the hand-wave dismissal? She linked her fingers together and lowered them onto her lap. She didn't want to go into details. No one, not even Dar, knew how bad her acrophobia was. She admonished herself for her lack of compassion and regained her composure, "Is she okay? Have you heard anything?" "I heard she said she couldn't breathe and blacked out. She's fine now. They released her after a few hours in the emergency room." He hesitated, "Could it've been something to do with oxygen levels?"

"I don't know. I'm checking that right now." She bent back toward the screen. She wondered the same thing. For the past week the oxygen levels in the atmosphere were giving random readings. Sometimes 20.5, then back to 20.6 or 20.7. And down again yesterday to 20.5. She monitored news blurbs every day in addition to medical reports from hospitals around the world. There seemed to be more and more reports of people collapsing from asphyxia. Lack of oxygen in the blood. It was random but she dug through reports and eyewitness accounts to see if there were any connections. Finding anomalies like this was a large part of the Institute's mission. She had been hoping by now that Yun would have some insight to the cause of the increased microbial activity and changes in the oxygen levels. He had been working tirelessly, leaving for just a few hours of sleep, and coming back. Almost as if it was a personal mission.

"By the way, what were you doing on that trail? You never go up there."

"Yeah, well, I was distracted. I think my head was focusing too much on work and what's been happening. I didn't notice where my feet were taking me." Sydney pushed herself from her desk. The wheels on the chair squeaked. "I've got a meeting in the main conference room in," she looked at the computer, "four minutes." She gathered papers. "Could you draw up some of the latest climatology reports?" Darweshi wasn't just a climatologist. He held a PhD in climate studies. Atmospheric weather patterns were his expertise. While his outward mannerisms might be flippant or perceived as less than meticulous, she trusted his work completely. Sydney needed to know if this recent oxygen level pattern was a blip or a trend. "Sure. I'll deliver them to you in the conference room." He wiped crumbs from his mouth with the back of his hand as he marched down the hall to his cubicle.

Sydney walked down the corridor, head down, scrolling through the latest medical reports. She did a full body slam into someone.

"Whoa. You need to watch where you're going."

It was Mark. "Sorry." She paused knowing she turned pink. Without looking up she scrambled around him toward the session with her mother. She had hired him two years ago.

His background was biogenetics and he was a prominent research scientist on genetic engineering. There was however, one, small detail - she had dated him while they both were at Harvard. After she hired him, she had promised herself to keep him at arms-length and conversations would only be business related. So far it had been working. She was out of the Stanford offices most of the year and would send him off on projects far from Stanford when she was back. However, she couldn't maintain that constant distance so, inevitably, when she saw him, something would flip inside her stomach making her uncomfortable.

This day started crappy and seemed to be staying that way.

Heading toward the conference room she started to make mental notes for the conversation with her mother. This project was going to require more support. At least one more person. The Earth Institute had thirty-seven employees along with several knowledge consultants engaged depending on a project's need. The current O$_2$ concern had Darweshi Kuhn, Li Yun and herself assigned. Sydney had worked nine years as the head geophysicist and, more importantly, managed the day-to-day operations. She oversaw project assignments, management of people and provided expertise in her field of study. She walked into the room determined to get her mother to agree to a knowledge consultant in microbiology. As soon as she sat down, Mark Connors walked in and sat opposite her at the conference table. While they were in graduate school, they had lived together. Two years ago, she had been surprised to see he had applied for a position at the Institute. He had lost his wife in a tragic accident that left him and their son, Ryan, without a mother. He now turned toward Sydney and nodded hello. He couldn't hide a slight smile probably from how she almost knocked him over a few minutes go.

"Why are you here?" She blurted out. Then trying to hide her annoyance she added in a softer tone, "and where's Dr. Davis?"

"She sent me a note this morning directing me to be here. I'm not sure."

"You're here because you'll be part of Sydney's team on the O_2 project." Dr. Davis announced as she walked to the head of the table. She remained standing. She turned toward Sydney with her hand out. "I need to see those latest reports on the oxygen levels."

"Darweshi will deliver them in a minute." Sydney regrouped. "Mark is a good candidate for the team," she started, attempting to be diplomatic, "but he is not an expert in microbiology." It didn't work. She said it with a bit too much emphasis. She struggled to hold back the anger. Anger at her mother for so much she didn't even know why anymore. Anger at Mark for witnessing her discomfort. She could feel her face burn. Out of the corner of her eye she saw him shift in his chair. He didn't look happy.

Darweshi saved her from total embarrassment by strolling in and waving the reports. "I'll take those." Dr. Davis grabbed the papers from Darweshi's hand. "I'll be in my office."

Mark didn't say a word. He got up and followed Dr. Davis out of the room.

Sydney dug her elbows into the table and dropped her forehead into her hands.

"So, I guess that was a quick update. Do you need something else?" Darweshi said.

FOUR

Mark held onto his self-control. He wasn't going to let Sydney's anger, frustration or whatever bothered her get to him. If Dr. Davis wanted him on this, he was going to be on it. He needed a coffee, black. He headed to the break room. He played back her dismissal of his genetics background. Didn't she know there is overlap between genetics and microbiology? As a matter of fact, there are many people working in those disciplines that could legitimately claim to be a geneticist and a microbiologist. Damn! She was a frustrating person. Of course she knew. He took a gulp of steaming coffee, yelled, and spit it into the sink. His tongue was on fire. Darweshi walked in and glanced in the sink. He went to the refrigerator and took a bottle of water, unscrewed the top and handed it to him.

Mark shook his head. "I'm fine." He wiped his mouth with a napkin. "I didn't expect it to be so hot." He made a motion to walk out, stopped and faced Darweshi. He didn't know Darweshi well but in the few dealings he had he found him to be an honest and straightforward person. "Dar, you've known Sydney for a long time, right?"

"Eight years or so."

"Did she ever tell you that we knew each other in graduate school, while we were both in Boston?" On the few occasions that Mark was at the Institute at the same time as Sydney he had seen Sydney and Darweshi break for lunch, either heading out to a local deli or meet in the Institute's lunchroom. Meanwhile his lunch breaks were spent heading back and forth to his small apartment to check on his son. Mark cherished those lunches when Ryan was in a calm mood and they each could enjoy precious time together.

"Yeah . . .umm . . . she mentioned it when she told me she hired you. It seemed like it was a good time of her life." Mark remained quiet. He felt his pulse quicken. After a few seconds Darweshi continued. "She doesn't go into any details." He took a gulp of water from the bottle. "Why, what's up?"

"She seems different now, that's all. Not the same person I knew back then. Of course, it was close to fourteen years ago." As he said this, he couldn't believe it was that long ago. He turned away and tried to sound nonchalant, "She seems so. . . ah, formal now. Don't get me wrong she was always very focused but she also laughed a lot. Had a fun side. Just wondered if anything happened. She changed."

Darweshi screwed the top back on the bottle. "Don't know. But don't we all?" Mark decided he wasn't going to get anywhere with this. He wondered why he even ca-red. "Yeah, we all change." He crumbled the napkin and threw it in the garbage as he walked out.

He hurried toward the parking lot. He had to take Ryan to his therapy session today. The woman, Dena, who he hired to watch Ryan, also needed the afternoon off. Mark welcomed attending the therapy sessions. Any amount of time he could devote to his son was another opportunity to bond. Dr. Judson said Ryan was making progress. When Mark's wife, Catherine, died two years ago, he thought Ryan would dissolve forever into his own world. Ryan was diagnosed as being on the spectrum when he was only four. By the time he was nine he had been acclimating so well to his classes at school that he started interacting with the teachers and other students. Ryan was even comfortable enough to take a series of tests. His counselor at school identified him as being exceptional on a scale for pattern recognition. Recognizing patterns in seemingly unrelated areas came easily to him. So easily in fact that he and Catherine made up a game about converging patterns. It seemed they both had that ability. In a sense their relationship went beyond mother-son. They both had a type of genius that connected them on another level. Then the accident happened and Ryan reverted to that boy who never spoke and hated to be touched. Catherine's death was devasting. Mark saw it as a miracle that he came upon Dr. Melvin Judson who was both an applied behavior and physical therapist. So far things were going well.

Mark pulled into the parking lot of their apartment complex. Dena was waiting on the stoop of the apartment building with Ryan sitting next to her. For an eleven-year-old, he was so small, so fragile. His head was turned toward the bricks of the building. The sun highlighted the curve of his profile. His light brown hair curled over his ear. He had his dad's deep hazel eyes which were focused on scratching out pieces of the brick's mortar with a stick. It never failed to tug at Mark's heart when he thought of how quickly Ryan retreated into himself after making so much progress. He silently prayed that today would be a breakthrough.

"Hey there, Ryan." Mark walked slowly. Ryan never liked swift movements.

"Thanks for coming early Dr. Connors. My sister's appointment will take the rest of the day. Is that okay?" Dena stood up. At sixty years old she was still strong and her manner was calm and reassuring. She was the perfect combination. Even a good cook. Mark was thankful for all she did for both Ryan and him.

"Yes, yes that's fine, Dena. I'll be here for the day. I'll see you tomorrow morning?"

"Yes." She stooped down and put her hand on Ryan's hand that still held the stick, "I'll see you, little man, tomorrow." She smiled down at him before walking to her car.

Ryan moved next to him. He took hold of his dad's pant leg and snuck a glance at his face.

Mark went down on one knee and put his arms around him. He was never sure of what kind of reaction he would get. So far today seemed to be a good day. "I'm so glad we'll have time together. Are you ready to go see Dr. Judson?"

"I am." Ryan's soft voice was barely audible.

CHAPTER

FIVE

Sydney sat in her office. It was the end of the day and she still had not heard from Yun. What was he doing? She had given him the assignment to determine the most likely factors for the increased microbial activity two days ago. She marched down to his work area. When she got there, he was in the middle of moving post-it notes from one part of his white board to another. And then he swapped them back again.

"Have you found something?" Sydney tried to make sense of all the notes on the white board. There appeared to be a map of the earth underneath all those orange and pink sticky notes. There was another color too. The green ones seemed to be concentrated in the northern hemisphere around Greenland.

Yun spun around. His energy was palpable. She could feel he was onto something.

"I had to prove your original hypothesis about the increased microbial activity in the northern hemisphere.

For my own sake, it was my first step. That's probably why it's taken me longer than you expected." He snuck a look at her before turning back to the board and pointing toward the green notes. "When I looked at the results from my tests, there definitely are increased microbes in the northern hemisphere, specifically around Greenland." He then went to his computer and pulled up a satellite image of a specific area in the northwest corner of the land mass in real-time.

Sydney pulled up a chair and studied what Yun displayed. It looked like large segments of rock, gravel, and ice pulling away from the mainland. As a geophysicist she knew about the dangers of melting glaciers. This looked more like land masses not glaciers. She had read some recent work on the permafrost deterioration. "Is this what I think it is? Permafrost melting?"

"Yes. But there's more. I had wanted to run some results again before reporting to you."

"I understand you want to make sure your work is perfect before giving it to me. But right now, and at the Institute in general, the most important thing is to report whatever you see, whenever you see it, no restrictions, no need to make it pretty." She wanted him to understand this is not a competition.

Yun nodded.

"Please go on. Tell me what your preliminary results show."

"I received samples of the water around the melting permafrost yesterday afternoon. I immediately ran tests to identify the microbes and compared that to a control sample." He dropped onto the chair next to her. "Looks like there're not only increased numbers in the sample but also unidentifiable bacteria. Approximately ten percent of the total are unidentified." He waited.

Sydney's mind kicked into high gear. Unidentified? What are they? How did they get there? A beat passed. And then her eyes opened wide. They were frozen! Frozen in the permafrost and now have been released into the arctic ocean. She kept quiet.

"I think there's something more about these specific bacteria that relate to the reduction of oxygen." Yun said. "It's not just the increased activity of the microbes." He started typing bringing up every strain of microbe that exists in the oceans today. "I'll look for research papers on these types of bacteria. Going back ten years or so."

Sydney couldn't stop her mind from jumping from different scenarios of what this meant. Would these prehistoric bacteria destroy sea life? Could this be the reason behind the oxygen depletion? But how? She knew the ramifications of one small change impacting a whole ecosystem. She needed time to think and didn't want to voice her thoughts – not yet anyway. She got up from the chair and mumbled, "I'll stop back later". Yun didn't look up. He was already on a mission, scanning screens at a breakneck speed.

She laid back her head on her office chair and stared up and out the window. Traces of the blue sky disappeared with the sun as it set. She could still feel the warmth on her skin. While her mother thought daydreaming was a waste of time, she knew it was a way for her creativity to blossom. She read once that the conscious brain stifled creativity. She believed it. As a scientist she followed the rules for finding the facts but even as a young girl she had a spark of something more. Something inside her that guided her. Some called it intuition. Others called it mindfulness. Twenty minutes later she bolted out of her chair and raced down the hallway. Yun was nowhere to be found. Where was he? Looked like he took a break. His coat was still on the back of his chair. She headed down the hallway hoping to find him in the break room. Not there. She went looking for Dar. His office was empty too. But he looked like he was gone for the day. Well, there's one person she knew would still be here. She steeled herself and sprinted up the stairs to the corner office.

Dr. Davis was on the phone. Her voice was raised shooting out non-stop questions that Sydney guessed didn't require an answer. She felt for the person on the other end. She stood on the threshold waiting.

Her mother ended the call with polite formality, "So good to speak with you Dr. Hu.

Please give my best to your family."

How does she do that? Switch gears in a nanosecond from a person you'd never want to see again in your life to your best friend in the world. Sydney had even tried it a few times.

Never worked.

"Yes?" Dr. Davis broke Sydney's thought.

"I've got something on that microbial activity."

"Well, what is it?"

"Yun found that ancient bacteria had been released as a result of permafrost melting on the coast of Greenland." Sydney sat down across from her mother. "He's now trying to determine if there's any evidence anywhere else on earth with these specific bacteria and if there's an impact on the ecology of the ocean."

"Did you get Mark involved?"

Sydney tried not to sound annoyed. "Not yet."

"He is the microbiologist on your team."

"Yes, I will. He had to take the afternoon off. I'll bring him up to speed as soon as he gets in tomorrow morning." She leaned forward putting both hands on the arms of the chair. She grappled with what she remembered when she was deep in thought and struggled with what it could mean. She shook her head not wanting to believe what she was about to say. She picked her head up. "It's the algae, mother. I read a paper once on the cycle of algae, a specific alga called diatoms. The cycle starts in the Sahara Desert and transverses the Atlantic to end up in the rainforests of the amazon basin. These diatoms supply the oxygen through photosynthesis for the rainforest."

"It's been a long day, Sydney. What are you saying? Diatoms have something to do with what's happening with the oxygen depletion?"

"Yes. Maybe. I know there is a connection. Here let me show you." Sydney got up and went to her mother's computer. She typed in diatoms and earth's atmosphere. Her mother hovered over her shoulder. They both silently skimmed through several recent journals. Sydney found a study completed last year regarding the impact of diatoms and the Amazon Basin.

Sydney's fingers froze over the keyboard as they both silently read the study's conclusion.

She looked at her mother who was looking down at the screen. Her mother put her finger against the screen, "Diatoms produce 50% of the earth's oxygen. Wait, 50%? I knew they were a factor, but 50%? If something happened to even a small percentage of these billions of organisms every living thing . . ." Her mother stopped. She didn't need to go any further.

SIX

· ·

Sydney collapsed on the edge of her bed. She knew that sleep was important. Her mind was always sharper and she was better able to cope with stress with a good night's rest. Her mother had remained at the office and called a few experts she knew in the field to gather more data.

Sydney hypothesized that somehow the diatoms were being destroyed by ancient bacteria. Before Sydney left for home, she had called the team. Mark said he'd be at the Institute as soon as he could in the morning. Both Dar and Yun said they'd meet her there by 6 a.m. The warm yellow light from a small lamp drew her attention to an old picture on her bureau. The bedroom was the only place she displayed nostalgia. It was of her and Aunt Rene. She was ten, holding a trophy, smiling from ear to ear. The award was for first place in the Future Earth Scientists contest. Aunt Rene had her arm around Sydney and looked so proud. She wasn't really an aunt but a good friend and colleague of her mother's. Sydney always knew she would be a scientist someday. Back then she wanted to be just like her mother. Admired. Intelligent. Focused. She found out later that her desire cost her dearly. She grew to accept that people found her aloof. Now as an adult she couldn't think of one person who was a true friend, well maybe Dar. And forget a love life, except for that brief time in college. She sighed, leaned over, switched off the light and pulled the covers over her.

The next morning she found Darweshi waiting for her at the office. Sleep had eluded her last night but Dar was clear-eyed. At least he got some sleep. "Good morning, Dar. Have you seen Yun yet?"

"No. Although I just got in."

"Let's head down to his workspace. I really wanted everybody together rather than talking about this one at a time." Sydney marched down the hall.

"What about Mark?" Darweshi turned toward Mark's office.

"He won't be here until later."

"I'm here." Mark's voice came from behind Sydney.

"Oh. Thought you couldn't get here till later." She kept walking toward Yun's office. "You said it was important, and I am a team player." He smiled just as she stopped to look at him.

"Right." Her face remained blank. Was he trying to get some reaction? She continued down the hall increasing her stride leaving Darweshi and Mark to catch up.

Yun was typing away and still had the white board up with colored sticky notes covering specific areas on the map. "Yun, please stop for a minute. I want to update everyone." Sydney relayed her thoughts and cited the journals she researched about diatoms and their environment.

Mark was the first to comment, "Diatoms? Infected?"

"Yes. I believe caused by ancient bacteria. It's just a hypothesis. There're no facts to support it yet." Sydney said.

Yun piped in. "I can set up an experiment to test this. I've requested samples of the bacteria from the permafrost melt. I'll also need to collect diatoms from the same location."

"Good. Mark, I'd like you to work on this with Yun." As soon as Sydney said this Yun pulled back from his computer. "Anything wrong, Yun?"

"No. no. That's fine. I'm used to working alone. That's all." He began typing again.

"Mark?"

"No problem. I'm fine working together."

"Dar, you continue to monitor the oxygen levels and report all anomalies. See if you can find out specific locations on the earth that have reduced oxygen. Particularly in the oceans. That's it. Let's get this figured out."

Sydney was halfway down the corridor when Mark raced up and kept pace with her.

"Are we okay? I mean are you good with me being on this as the microbiologist?"

"It's not important if I'm good with you being on the O$_2$ team. Dr. Davis is right. You're the perfect person with your expertise." Sydney said as she slowed down.

"But I want to know how you feel about it." Mark went to touch her arm.

Sydney's foot caught something on the carpet breaking her stride. Mark's hand caught her. Sydney's stomach felt empty. She pulled away, "My feelings don't come into play here."

CHAPTER
SEVEN

Yun wasn't happy. A few days had passed since Mark began working with him. Yun didn't need someone looking over his shoulder. He kept up with the required work while still having time to work on his side project. The corners of his mouth turned up as he thought of his brilliant idea to disguise the software app as a game. Yun closed the lid to his laptop. His legs tingled as he rose from the chair he'd been sitting in for over nine hours. His hand instinctively went to rub the feeling back into his backside. Today was a long one but it was all worth it. He was spending every night this week secretly coming into the building to work on the game. And during the day he was what everyone expected him to be – the brilliant child-prodigy working on a special project for a famous Institute in California. No one suspected he was anything but that nerdy kid with a doctorate in evolutionary botany. He snuck out of the dark building and headed home to get at least three hours of sleep.

At ten the next morning he hurried past the guard barely flashing his photo ID. He was late. Unfortunately, he didn't go unnoticed.

"Yun. Hold up for a second."

"Damn." He muttered under his breath and spun around to face her. "Good morning, Dr. Davis." He forced his perfect smile and his jet-black hair flopped across his eye.

"I understand you've been working late. One of the guards saw you leave during the early morning hours for two days in a row."

He didn't hesitate, "Oh yeah. I get so involved in the work that I lost track of time. Guess I should've set an alarm." He shrugged and hoped she'd accept the lame excuse.

"Yes, well," She looked him up and down, "from now on if you work late let security know."

Yun nodded. She seemed to accept his excuse and continued walking in the opposite direction. He headed up the stairs to his office. The game was just about done. He called it *Surrection*. Anyone who opened it would think it was a simple game of world-building with magic rooms, impossible obstacles, and special weapons where the avatars would fight each other for control and dominance. But it wasn't.

Beneath the game was a sophisticated communication and monitoring app. All one had to do is link to one of the zillion satellites orbiting earth. A secure line would be established directly to a secret facility in the Indian Ocean. Yun was almost there. When he finished, no one would guess he would be doing something other than playing a game on his machine. He was clocking in almost twenty hours per day, but so far so good. He smiled as he bent over to type.

"How's it going?" Mark stood at the doorway. "I've gotten some results from the diatom samples in other parts of the arctic ocean."

Yun stopped typing and blanked out his screen. He didn't respond.

"What about your results from the samples along the coast of Greenland around where the permafrost melted?" Mark said walking closer to Yun.

Yun shook his head. "Yes, yes. Just now. I was reviewing before reporting."

"What have you found?"

"Over forty percent of the sample is dead. It looks like the unidentified bacteria has penetrated the diatoms single cell wall and infected the organism."

"Forty? Wow. Much more than what I found. In the southern part of the arctic there is a death rate of twenty-seven percent. Thirty-two near the north pole. We're calling the unidentified bacteria '*Greenlanium diatus*'. For now, anyway." Mark ran his hand over the top of his head. "We need to get Sydney." Mark walked away and said over his shoulder, "Gather all your numbers. I'll find Sydney and bring her back."

Yun touched the metal coin under his shirt. He had put it on a chain hung around his neck since his brother Chin had given it to him almost six years ago. The pain when Chin left didn't soften but rather hardened his resolve.

He vowed he would do his part as he'd promised his brother that day so long ago.

Sydney stood in Darweshi's office as her scientific mind kicked into overdrive. She gripped Dar's shoulder with one hand as she hunched over his screen.

"I've been looking for you." Mark said and walked over to them, "I was with Yun and . . "

"Mark, look here. Look at this." She pointed to an image of the north pole. There were several numbers in the right-hand corner.

"What am I looking at?"

"Those are fluctuation variations around the north pole." Darweshi explained.

"Fluctuations of the magnetic field that protects earth from the sun's radiation."

Sydney paced with tightened fists against her sides. "This happened about an hour ago. Dar was working on gathering information on the ocean levels of oxygen when he discovered unusual readings in the North Atlantic."

Darweshi typed in a few more numbers on the screen. The North Pole was replaced by a wide-angle view of the earth from two hundred miles above the surface. The delicate thin blue line of the atmosphere glowed. "This isn't right." He read through a list of numbers across the page. "The radiation levels in the area above the pole changed." He typed in more calculations. This time flashing red numbers appeared. "Wait a sec. There's been a major shift in the magnetic poles."

"What do you mean a shift?" Mark said.

"It's something that happens and has been happening over the course of earth's history. Earth's magnetic field has been slowly changing throughout its existence."

"Then what's the problem?" Mark hovered over Dar and leaned in.

Sydney raced over and stood on the other side of Dar and pointed to the set of numbers in the right corner. Her finger lightly touched the screen and immediately pulled back like they were burned. "These blinking red numbers are radiation levels." She didn't or couldn't believe it.

"The shift caused a momentary breach in the atmosphere allowing the sun's radiation to come through," Darweshi confirmed. "The earth was exposed for about", he looked down at his watch, "forty-two seconds. In this area around the pole." He made a circle with his finger outlining a radius that covered part of Greenland.

Mark stepped back. "That means contamination. How bad is it?"

"Can't tell yet. But guaranteed anything living there was exposed." Darweshi stiffened and rolled away from the screen.

"I was just with Yun. The diatoms in that location have been infected. More than 40% have bacterial infections." Mark turned to Sydney. "What's happening here?"

The room went silent.

CHAPTER
EIGHT

December 14, 2039

Stanford, CA

Sydney had told them everything. No sense in holding back. They were all in it from the beginning and deserved to know. She reached for the glass of water on the conference table. Her team surrounded her, all eyes waiting for something more, something she couldn't give them, good news. She took a sip and rested the glass back down. As the December wind battered the large windows, she could feel their collective breath stall in anxious anticipation. There was an aura of disbelief, of confusion. It was only three days ago that they had discovered the devastating causes of the diatom destruction. Not only had an ancient bacteria penetrated the single cell organism but the thing that catapulted the timeframe to a red emergency alert was the leak of the sun's radiation in that same area. Diatom reproduction stopped. The oxygen depletion was back down to 20.5% and even more terrifying, there was no indication that it was going to return to normal. She'd spent hours running predictive analysis on the consequences. No matter how many times she checked and rechecked, at this rate her prediction held firm that within a year humans would not be able to survive the depleted earth's atmosphere. She pushed away an even more chilling thought; could some people already be dying?

Darweshi, his dark brown eyes opened wide, broke the silence, "Wait a minute. What are you saying? A year? That's crazy."

She knew he didn't mean to be flippant. He was the oldest member of the team, yet he often acted much younger, especially when upset. And even though he provided much of the data for her prediction of a year, she knew he found this impossible to fathom. She could feel him waiting for her to say something, that it was all a mistake. Unfortunately, there was nothing else.

"I know it sounds unbelievable," Sydney circled back toward her chair, "I have revisited every model and the timeframe is valid."

Dr. Davis entered the room just as Sydney sat in her chair tucking her chin and gazing down. Dr. Davis carried her tall frame rigid across the room before bending at the waist to lean her hands on the table. The sun at her back from the large windows cast an intimidating shadow across the room. "It's true. What Sydney revealed is not a theoretical possibility nor assumption. It's fact. And because of the critical consequences of this information, it's listed as highly confidential and not to be discussed with anyone outside this group." Her delivery was blunt, almost threatening.

Her mother had always handled the money and political end while she immersed herself with the team. But not this time. Her mother insisted she be part of the discussions with the international committees and leaders of the world. Sydney watched her mother move to a chair and wondered how she managed to stay aloof and controlled in this situation. She, on the other hand, couldn't stop her thoughts from taking off into a rabbit hole of unspeakable consequences. She shifted in her chair and crossed her legs as she listened to her mother. They had both returned last night from DC. It was a draining day. During the session, the Institute was chosen to head up a first phase approach for combating the crisis.

Mark sat, elbows on at the conference table, and massaged his temples. He turned toward Sydney and stared at her furrowing his brow. "It all happened so fast. I mean I know scientists have studied the reduction of oxygen since the early 2000s. Research since then consistently predicted oxygen depletion, but hundreds of years into the future." He shook his head, "If I wasn't here and part of this, actually seen it with my own eyes, I don't think I could've believed it."

Sydney drew her fingers through her hair. "I'm as shocked as you."

Darweshi loosened the shirt collar around his neck. "Most people won't even know they are slipping away. Like when explorers hike up mountains without enough oxygen."

Mark raised his voice. "Wait a sec. What about all life on earth? This prediction impacts every living thing."

"Yes, it does." Dr. Davis said.

"The Institute has been asked to design a high-level fail-safe for humans." Sydney said. "Of course, there are many other organizations involved. We all have a part. Each organization has been tasked with looking into different species, encompassing all living organisms on earth."

Her mother chimed in. "In addition, there is a separate group of scientists charged with coming up with a solution to destroy the bacteria, '*Greenlanium diatus*', and regrow diatoms. Stabilize them to their normal rate of growth." She coughed into her hand. "But that will take longer than . . ." She waved her hand.

Yun sat with his head folded down between his shoulders. His hair flopped over his face covering his eyes, making him look like a sullen teenager.

At that moment Sydney internalized everything about the Institute and what it represented. 'Earth – Protect and Respect' those words inscribed above the entrance. She thought of why she dedicated her life to the Institute. About how everything she believed in would now be tested. She wondered if she could hold up. There was no doubt that her passion and capabilities excelled when in a team but she was not good at handling politics, nor making speeches. She sat forward. Her words broke the silence, "Impossible as it may seem right now, there is a solution." The wind banged against the windows as if to compel them into action. "Go home and put your personal lives on hold. Get prepared. Do whatever you have to do to spend every waking hour working on this. We'll regroup early tomorrow." Sydney glanced at her mother before collecting her notes from the table. She managed to hold herself steady as she headed for the door.

As she walked out, she caught Yun's words, "The earth has finally said, 'Enough!'"

CHAPTER
NINE

• •

Sydney needed to clear her head. As soon as she left the conference room, she grabbed her coat and went outside to the sloping paths of the campus. It was five p.m. She pulled her collar against the cold air, picking up her pace. Twilight had set in offering a stunning view of the city lights against the coast of California. She never tired of it.

Exhaustion was overpowering but she felt compelled to run. It would revive her mind and body. When she got back to her office, she closed the blinds then changed into sweats and pulled on a knit cap. After tying her shoelaces, she clicked on a classic rock track from Taylor Swift and headed outside. Running had been her outlet and passion since college days. Her tall frame and lanky body fell easily into a stride. As she ran through the pathways around the buildings her mind reeled through visuals of devastation.

"Dammit." She stopped short. Her feet had taken her to the edge of the cliff. She jumped backwards. Nothing relieved the anxiety she felt when she looked down into a vastness. She was resigned that a fear of heights would always be part of her make-up. As she walked back to the offices an idea that had started days ago when she first discovered the results scratched the surface of her brain. This time leaving the inkling of an actual proposal. She picked up her pace.

Sydney burst into her mother's office. Her mother glanced up over her glasses as she continued working on her computer. She wasn't mom, or even Ann. Mother was always Dr. Davis, strong-willed and uncompromising. As scientific partners, they were a relentless force, but the mother-daughter connection was non-existent. As a young child Sydney couldn't recall a day that made her feel that warm fuzziness from a mother's care. Her friends' mothers would kiss scraped knees and carefully place bandages over bruises while she watched from a distance.

"As I was running, I went over it again," Sydney began. "The whole disruption of earth's biology and environments that led us here," she strode back and forth to release the pent-up frustration and gather her thoughts. Her mother gave her a 'I don't have time for this' look. Sydney ignored it. "The major destruction of whole ecosystems, so closely aligned, impacted the natural order. Everything that happened during those early climate-change years instigated gradual damages to the future of the earth. Damages that were never understood."

Dr. Davis let out a long sigh, "Yes, unfortunately now with the discovery of the sudden decrease in diatoms it's too late to react. That decrease piled with the devastation of trees, specifically in the Amazon basin, all became triggers in the disruption of oxygen in the atmosphere."

"Exactly." She looked out the window at the clouds racing across the face of the moon. "We were paying so much attention to the carbon dioxide threat that we missed the near-term impact on oxygen levels. We thought we had time." Her mother may have lacked compassion and lord knows she had no motherly instincts but she more than made up for it with her brilliant mind. This was the one part of their relationship she enjoyed. The feeding off each other. Sydney added, "There must be a way we can control the next sequence of events by dealing with the depletion of oxygen in a different way. Perhaps by adjusting how humans breathe."

"What are you saying? As we discussed, there are others concentrating on the regrowth of diatoms and seeding the atmosphere. Our purpose in all this is to find a way to save as many humans as possible while the other teams of scientists determine the path forward and enact it." Davis said as she spread her fingers out and opened her arms.

Sydney faced her mother, "Every change to our fragile earth is injurious these days. As we know, the earth, like every living organism, has its own locked in, DNA sequences."

"Yes, and . . ."

Sydney interrupted and placed her hand on her mother's desk, "During my run I had an idea."

CHAPTER
TEN

Hours later, Sydney was back in her office. By three a.m. she outlined a rough plan. This couldn't wait another minute. She pinged Mark's phone.

"I have something. Dr. Davis and I've been working on it all night. I can't sleep. I need to talk with you, Darweshi, and Yun as soon as possible," she said without taking a breath.

"Sydney?" He yawned. She knew he hated the latest communication technology. He was an old-fashioned type, eventually adapting to new technology. He couldn't stand that the Institute required a com-chip be implanted behind his ear. In the past she had teased him about it. He had given her one of his stern looks – the one with the crunched-up forehead and tight lips. She smiled to herself remembering.

"Yes, yes. It's me. Can you contact Dar and Yun? Meet me at the Institute in an hour."

Having Mark on her team stirred up memories at the most inopportune time. The thought that she'd interrupted his sleep sent memories surging through her like a storm. The first time she met him pushed its way forward. She had been a sophomore at Harvard and he, a graduate student.

Boston had logged the coldest winter on record that year and it was just January. Sydney could kick herself. Why had she signed up for a swim class? What was she thinking? It was smack in the middle of her two most critical not to mention mind-consuming classes, analytical chemistry, and advanced calculus. She vaguely remembered thinking it would be a calming interlude or even an antidote to those two brain-bending hours. It wasn't. The combination of an icy cold wind off the Charles and the ridiculous physical distance between the swim center and the science labs only added to her anxiety when she realized she had to know how to swim to take an artistic swim class. Her mother in her typical uninterested way never paid much attention to Sydney's athletic education. As a result, she never learned to swim or play any team sports. In mother's mind why would a scientist need to know how to play anything.

As she had left the chemistry lab that day, the wind howled through the quad forming ice-encased branches on the delicate birches. She held her wool scarf around her neck and began the fifteen-minute run while her overstuffed backpack bounced against her spine. She was always the last one to arrive at the pool. As she sped up to make the corner around the last building, a revved-up motor and flash of something red cut her off. She slid on a piece of ice, almost losing her balance, and jumped back to avoid a collision.

"Hey, those have to stay in the safety lanes!" She shouted at her assailant. He had stopped a few feet in front of her. His motor spinner rumbled and whined from the sudden stop. He turned it off and straddled it between his legs. "Are you okay?"

"You're not supposed to be riding one of those here." Motor spinners available to any student on campus may be convenient but she considered them a menace. You pick up one and drive to another location and leave it for another student. She hated them and never considered using one. Her ears and cheeks were hot with frustration. Now she was going to be very late.

"I'm sorry. Are you okay?" He hopped over the crimson spinner and crouched down by her side and grabbed her backpack which fell to the ground. "You were in the spinner lane," he cautiously admonished.

The wind had formed tiny crystals of ice on his unprotected face, especially the eyebrows which framed a pair of intense green eyes. "I'm fine." Sydney snatched her backpack out of his grasp. "And I was not in your lane." She took a quick look at the neon yellow markings on the ground. She was standing in its center. "Well maybe, but you came right at me!"

"I didn't see you. You came around that corner like you were being chased by a bear or something." She didn't back away as he took a step closer.

"I'm late for class." He was a head taller than her. She stood staring at his face with her chin lifted.

"Must be a pretty important one." His eyes crinkled as the corners of his mouth came up.

"Swim class," she glanced at the time on her phone, "but I'm so late now." To herself she muttered, "Maybe I'll go to the library for an hour." He had moved even closer. She jumped back. She couldn't stop looking at his face.

"Hop on. I'll give you a ride over there." She stiffened. He held his hands up in surrender and laughed. "I promise not to kidnap you." It was a bright full laugh.

Sydney brushed past him. "Another time."

He hopped back on the spinner and turned around to face her, "I'm Mark, by the way." Her eyes had followed him as he sped off in the opposite direction and disappeared around a building.

That was so many years ago, but the memory stirred long-buried feelings.

CHAPTER
ELEVEN

Mark scratched his chin and got out of bed. This was not the first time Sydney had called and disturbed a good night's sleep. Her dedication to the Institute was consuming her life. As far as he knew she had no friends, just colleagues. Although, he understood she had something to prove. A mother like Ann Davis would make the strongest personality tremble from fear of not being good enough. The time when they were together in college he had broken through Sydney's shell and found a funny and caring person. Granted it was buried deep but back then he would have done anything for her. He had loved her. He shook his head at the thought of how she left. She had never said she loved him, but he was sure, up to that day anyway, that she did.

"Mother called this morning and has a position at the Institute." She had been walking out of the steamed-up bathroom of the tiny apartment they had shared in Cambridge. The brick building was built in the 1700's and the cold February wind snuck through every crack. She smelled fresh from her shower and had on his wool sweater that brushed against her bare thighs. Her hair was tied up in a towel.

"What kind of position?" Mark said. He was preoccupied with his dissertation and studying notes spread across the small bed.

"Head of Development. Directly under her."

He brought his eyes up to hers. She looked away.

"It's exactly what I want. Perfect, in fact."

"Oh?"

"Don't."

"Don't what?"

"Try to make me feel guilty. I'm going. I've made up my mind."

She never explained why. They had argued for days about her decision to go. When she finally left, he was sure she would return. He called. He sent notes. She had cut him off completely. He thought she wanted a family. Late night discussions included shared dreams of having children. After two difficult years he gave up those dreams. He opened his life again, met Catherine, and now had Ryan whom he loved more than anyone.

Mark went into the bathroom and started the shower. He quickly got dressed and greeted Dena arriving as he walked out of the house knowing he would do everything in his power to make this world safe for his son.

CHAPTER
TWELVE

Sydney, Darweshi, Yun, Mark, and Dr. Davis gathered in the same conference room. The room still had an air of disbelief, of dread filling the corners. Sydney stood and relaxed her shoulders. From this point forward she promised herself nothing would get in her way. She would be as ruthless as her mother. "Our work here has always been crucial to maintaining a healthy planet. Critical, in fact, in so many ways. We have been instrumental in providing research on environmental issues and consulting with governments and facilitating discussions. Now we get to do more than just put together impact analysis. Based on the facts presented yesterday, Dr. Davis and I did some brainstorming and came up with a proposal." She sat down, "After our meeting ended, I went for a run to clear my head and concentrated on my breath. This helps to calm me, like meditation. This time it also reminded me of a marathon in the Rockies several years ago." In truth, it was the nearness of that cliff she almost ran off that reminded her of that treacherous race. Sydney saw Mark shifting in his chair and pushing his thick brown hair off his forehead. Always impatient. "The marathon went up to thirteen thousand feet. The runners exposed at that elevation on a consistent basis were able to process the air. They never had issues with their breath." Mark continued to fidget. "But I had issues with breathing during the race. It made me think, there are people that live in environments with less oxygen all the time and their bodies have adapted to the lower levels of oxygen."

Mark sat upright his mouth half opened. She knew that would get him. She sensed he knew where she was headed.

Darweshi spoke with eyes half-closed. "So, what do you think? How do we help everyone else who doesn't live at thirteen thousand feet? Maybe start an oxygen store business?" Along with acting a lot younger he also managed his anxiety by off-handed humor.

Dr. Davis removed her glasses, "We change their DNA."

Sydney snapped her head around. This was her moment and once again her mother robbed her. As if water had splashed in her face she shook remembering when she had won the Respected Young Scientist Award at an impressive young age of eleven. She had stood on the podium accepting her trophy beaming with pride. She had never expected her mother to show at any of these events. Dr. Davis was either doing speaking tours or consulting with heads of state or businesses for most of her youth. But at this event, at that precise moment, her mother had come, striding down the aisle of the auditorium like it was the red carpet. The entire audience had clapped. Sydney never knew if it was for her or her mother.

Sydney tamped down her knee-jerk anger and focused on Mark. As the bio-geneticist his opinion was critical. His credentials included discoveries in genetic function and transmission of genes. He had won the prize from the Gruber Foundation.

"You're talking about redesigning people," Mark said. He put both hands on the table and pulled back in his chair. "Certainly feasible, but ethical? Not to this extent. I have a feeling there will be safety regulations and global authorities standing in your way. And it's not a longterm solution unless you are considering changing the DNA in embryo cells or including a genetic engine within the cells. Having a genetic engine would change those cells automatically, creating this 'new' DNA for humans as a race. Which, by the way, is emphatically forbidden by any standard of scientific ethics."

"Hold on. How does this human edit work?" Darweshi said.

Dr. Davis waved her hand. "Think of it more like using a basic word processing editor, only for genes. Our DNA is a sequence of four letters combined in groups. Replace this letter with that one." Davis turned back toward Mark. She had picked up on Mark's last comment and her voice became louder and faster. "Why can't we edit the embryo cells? That would guarantee the changed DNA would pass on from generation to generation. Humans would require less oxygen to breath. That would be the long-term solution instead of regrowing and infusing diatoms back into the atmosphere. It would be such a coup for me if we had the solution. I . . . um. . . the Institute should be written in the history books with this global DNA edit."

Everyone in the room stopped and looked at Dr. Davis. Sydney leaned forward. "We need to think this through. First, we must process the idea of a gene edit of this magnitude. It has never been done before."

Mark's calm, low-tenor voice addressed Dr. Davis. "Implementing a genetic engine wouldn't work in this case. Because of the human reproductive cycle, it would take generations to become effective across the globe. By then humans would have succumbed to the lack of oxygen. The best solution must be to infuse diatoms back into the cycle of earth's atmosphere." He looked at Sydney. "But your idea for specific gene editing could be a short-term answer. Especially if time is a constraint. With the technology today we may be able to come up with a genetic sequence in a week or two."

Several hours later of back-and-forth discussion, Dr. Davis acquiesced to the scientific reality of what was viable and more importantly, would not raise any ethical issue. Gaining global consensus was paramount. Dr. Davis concluded, "All right then, I will report that the Institute will provide a plan that can be implemented in a week, two at the most. Once we have the genetic solution it then would be a matter of producing it on a large scale and administering it to the world's population. Like a vaccine for a pandemic. If we can get this accomplished, our gene edit will be a stop gap until the global plan to increase diatoms is in place."

Sydney nodded, "According to my calculations once there is a method to regrow diatoms, getting the atmosphere to reverse to increasing oxygen will take at least six months. People will start dying of asphyxiation as soon as a month from now, at least those most vulnerable. We need to adopt a plan and move on it. Now." What Sydney didn't say was that she intended to check reports from around the world for deaths due to lack of oxygen. Without telling anyone, she had created a global search that would identify any cases of death that were related to asphyxia. The initial results would be coming in today.

Mark scratched his chin and stood, "Scientist have been working with many human genetic editing tools that could potentially do this. CRISPR is one and probably the oldest." Then quickly added, "But the harder part is finding a social group whose DNA could be used as a blueprint. The key for genetic edits is to target where you want the changes to occur in the genes and how. That's the map. The blueprint. Then we would be able to format people's genes to the correct sequence." Mark voice got louder. He went over to Yun who was typing on the computer, "What about finding a group of people, like the runners you described in the Rockies? People who can already function at lower levels of oxygen. Or people like Sherpas, who live in the Himalayas?"

Yun listened quietly and continued tapping keys on his computer. Dr. Davis stood next to Mark and looked over Yun's shoulder. She told him to bring up geographic locations with the highest elevations that are permanent settlements. "It's important that the location be a place where people have lived for at least a century. We want to have the highest probability that the people are genetically adapted to the high elevation." Yun kept silent as his eyes locked onto the screen and his fingers raced across the keyboard.

Sydney watched as they all gathered around Yun. She had not done the same extensive background review on him as she had with the rest of the team. While his education was unparalleled for someone so young, she knew nothing else about him. And now he was in the thick of it. She had revealed to Mark that she had a hard time investigating Yuns' years before graduate school when he was in China. She had been intent on the follow up, but then this happened.

CHAPTER
THIRTEEN

A s they continued discussing the location for the testing, Yun blocked them out. The conversation became a low din in the back of his consciousness. His mind was free to turn to something else. Something he promised he would do but never knew how it would manifest. Now he did. He reached toward his neck but didn't touch it. He could feel the coin. It was always with him. Chin, at the age of sixteen, had struck out on his own to join an environmental activist group. With nothing much to do in the very poor and mostly abandoned area of China, Chin was the perfect recruit. Even as a young child his brother had been obsessed with the devastations caused by poisonous chemicals to their local environment and found allies who felt the only way to cause change was through the destruction of major offenders. Yun lived with his brother, mother and father in an apartment overlooking the Yangtze River where the sounds of the street vendors during the day and the gangs at night kept them company. Yun stared out over the keyboard as he remembered the afternoon Chin left.

"It's from the Qing Dynasty. Not worth a lot of money but it has powers. I want you to have this." In the dimly lit bedroom that they had shared, Chin held the coin up for Yun to examine. It was a round coin with a square hole in the center. "The round shape represents heaven, and the square represents earth. Do you see? It's one coin but separate manifestations of the same space. I'm leaving today and want you to remember that no matter what happens, one day we will both be together again. Like this coin whether we are in heaven or earth."

Yun had been reaching out to take the coin then drew his hand back. "But where are you going? You can't leave." Tears stung Yun's eyes. He forced them back not wanting Chin to see his weakness. None fell on his cheeks. Yun puffed out his chest. "I'll go with you."

Chin shook his head. "You must be brave. Braver than anyone else and I must do this on my own. One day you'll know your destiny." As Chin grabbed Yun for a final embrace, he placed the coin in Yun's back pocket. "Promise me that you will find your cause, your purpose in this life. And remember that people may have to die to fulfil that purpose." He stepped back and held Yun at arm's length "Promise me."

Yun could think of nothing else to say to make his brother stay. "Yes, yes, I promise."

He had come to understand what those last words from his brother meant.

CHAPTER
FOURTEEN

Sydney setup a room where everyone worked side by side. Working this way each person could communicate immediately and she could monitor progress without pausing her own work. By eight a.m., exhausted but still combing through research on CRISPR and gene editing, Sydney saw Mark get up from his computer. "I need to get Ryan. I left him with my sister last night. I'll pick him up and come right back. He'll be with me all day, is that okay?"

Sydney knew Mark's son. Or more accurately, she met him once at an Institute annual picnic. Ryan was eleven and diagnosed with autism spectrum disorder. She knew a bit about it. Ryan had delayed speech patterns and, when he did speak, it was a whisper to Mark. That and his repetitive behavior of shrugging his shoulders were the outward signs she noticed. What she also noticed was Mark's dedication to Ryan. She could tell from the first moment when she saw them together. What would her life have been like if she'd stayed with Mark? She shook off the thought and replied, "As long as you are available when we need you."

Later that afternoon Sydney noticed Mark's return and nodded as he led Ryan to a table with a computer. Ryan began playing video games and seemed entranced by the graphics. Mark slowly made his way back to his desk. Just then Yun jumped up off his chair. "I found it." He rubbed his lower back. Mark rolled his chair over to view Yun's screen. Yun tilted it for Mark to see. "Right here. It's perfect. Everything we are looking for."

Sydney and Dar sprung up from Yun's excitement and both positioned themselves looking over Mark's shoulder. She placed her hand on the back of the chair lightly touching Mark's shirt. Yun sat back down and pointed at a map of Peru. "It's at least 18,000 feet and has had a settlement there since the Incas. It's not a tourist place and has some type of industry, gold mining, I think." Yun scrolled through the pages of information.

Mark stopped Yun when a picture of a giant glacier appeared. It overshadowed a small village below it. "Looks sort of primitive, doesn't it?"

Sydney patted Yun's shoulder, "Great job, Yun. La Rinconada. This looks promising. We'll need a full work up and gather as much information as you can on the population, social climate, government and corporations, culture, etc. Get back to me in a few hours." Sydney looked to Mark, "Can you spend time with Yun on this?" Already planning the next steps, she didn't wait for his reply. She would send Darweshi to La Rinconada tomorrow to prepare the location and coordinate the supplies and equipment they would need. Her mind switched to concentrate on the logistics of building a lab at 18,000 feet in the Andes. They would need a thermocycler, centrifuges, refrigeration units and some high processing computers for the software. The full DNA sequence software would be the baseline. But finding the gene you wanted to modify and inserting the information into a cell? - that was going to be the delicate part requiring a steady human hand and razor focus.

Sydney felt relieved to have an actual location. If there were no major setbacks in the review from Mark and Yun, they would all be in La Rinconada by next week. She went back to her office. She needed to check the climatology reports and hoped the results from her global search had come in. Who knew if or when the oxygen levels could start decreasing faster than anticipated? She kept her fears, and the number of deaths from asphyxiation to herself. She needed to stay focused.

Late in the day, Mark approached Sydney. "Everything looks promising with La Rinconada. The only thing is I couldn't gather much about a company there. They are privately held. But what I do know is their business is gold mining and they own a major mine in the town. I did some research to get names of the top guys. I found a Fred Hotchkiss. He's in public relations. I ca…"

"Did you call him?" She dug her fingers into her temples. It was a nervous habit since she was a child.

Mark nodded. "I did. He delivered a prepared speech about the gold mine, like a robot. But I could tell by the slight hesitation in his voice when I mentioned our classified project that he was concerned. He couldn't give me much information and specifically nothing to help us get approvals to do research on the property. And we may even get pushback, especially since we can't reveal what we're really doing. Also, it sounded like the company is run by one man, Wallace Katen, who has final say about everything that happens in La Rinconada."

"Let me work out the approvals we'll need from Wallace Katen."

The next day was a blur. Sydney ended up relying on her mother's influence to get Katen's approval for her team to use a warehouse on his company's property.

Dr. Davis sat in her office that evening. "I'm glad you came to me. Wallace Katen was an extremely hard person to get hold of. But I did. I have connections with the international gold conglomerate, and I know people."

"Right. Well, thank you mother for getting this done so quickly." Sydney blew out a breath, trying to keep her temper in check. At times she had no idea where her anger came from. "I'll take care of everything else from here on out. I'm sending Darweshi to La Rinconada today." Sydney walked out. She hoped one day her stomach wouldn't churn when she was around her.

Sydney spent much of the day planning for the Andes trip and mapping out the timeline. It would take two days to get to La Rinconada. Once there, she'd allocate one day for final lab setup and two days for the collection of the cells for the blueprint DNA. After that it was a matter of creating the DNA injections and testing it on subjects. She figured they would have what they needed for general population distribution within six, maybe seven days. The stats on La Rinconada reported just under two hundred people living in a two square mile development. The locals living there were descendants of the

Incas. The team would be collecting their DNA as the blueprint for the CRISPR injections. She held her head in her hands and shut her eyes. She considered the potential weaknesses in the plan. They assumed the blueprint DNA from the people in La Rinconada was truly the reason for their ability to breath lower oxygen levels. And, of course, there was the possibility the locals might refuse to give their DNA. This could be a delicate situation that must be handled carefully and with consideration of the people in La Rinconada. The other areas of concern revolved around the unknowns of the actual environment. She had read that the settlement is remote and doesn't have modern technology. In addition, the spiritual practices in that region are pervasive. Not a good combination for a scientific based 'save the world' experiment. All of these, direct and indirect possibilities for failure, kept her mind on edge. The apprehension became a constant burning sensation. By three p.m., she received information regarding the search she had run. It was not what she had hoped. There was a high probability that at-risk people were dying from lack of oxygen. Two cases were confirmed as death by asphyxiation. One in Beijing and one in Chicago, Ill.

CHAPTER
FIFTEEN

* *

Human Oxygen Deprivation Deaths (h-ODD) 2
Oxygen level 20.5

Mark paced around Sydney's small office. She couldn't bear that his broad frame along with his booming voice occupied most of the space. He bumped into the corner of her desk each time he turned around, his fists tight. "I've talked with Dr. Davis and she's fine with Ryan coming along."

"Fine? Really." Sydney suddenly recalled all the times she had to beg to come along on work trips with her mother.

"Okay, not fine exactly. But in the end, she approved."

Sydney sat at her desk and felt like tripping him as he bumped into it once more. "Dr. Davis has approved? Well now, I guess that's it then!" She threw up her arms. She shook her head and pointed to her chest, "I'm the lead on this. Why didn't you come to me?" She waited a second and before he had time to answer, "I know why. It's because I would've said we absolutely cannot have your son on this trip. We're heading to one of the most remote locations in the world. So, whether Dr. Davis gave her approval or not, I cannot sanction bringing Ryan."

How dare he blindside her? The team had worked tirelessly. Preparations were finally in place. Sydney was familiar with Mark's flashes of outrage. She had witnessed it firsthand. He was a crusader for the weak and for people that could not help themselves. She realized with an ASD child this natural tendency would be magnified. Back then she had been drawn to his powerful feelings of protecting the rights of people. Sydney remembered how she had embraced his passion and, as if magic dust was just sprinkled over her, she felt herself relax into the chair. The energy of her movement quieted the room.

Mark put his hands in his pockets. "Listen. When Ryan lost his mother, he suffered from an extreme type of grieving. He can get quite intense, physical even." He stood still by her desk. "I'm the only one who can calm him down when he gets that way." His hand came out of his pocket and went to the back of his neck massaging the muscles. "He was so close to Catherine. They were joined by a special bond."

Sydney's eyes rested on his face.

He let out a long sigh. "Catherine used to play a game with him she made up called 'and what happens next?'. Either one of them would start the game by devising a scenario. It could be anything from a simple social interaction like two friends meeting on the street, to a comet hurdling through space. Once the first person created the scene the other would build on it. But it wasn't just a random process. It was a predictive, scientific one, based on patterns. Ryan inherited his mother's ability for pattern recognition, but I never realized that his ability was beyond exceptional. It's game theory. An area of science that can be applied to everything. What he can do is incredible."

Sydney processed what Mark revealed but wasn't sure where he was going. "Wait a second. Do you mean he can model a strategic projection using mathematical calculations? I know game theory is basic in economics, but he does it with everything?"

"Yes, and all in his head. I've done so much reading on ASD. Do you know there is a genius link with ASD on the genome?"

"Amazing." Sydney had heard he had a gift, but never inquired. "And you think Catherine had that genius link?"

Mark nodded. "Catherine was a talented woman. She could have done anything. She decided to go into social work, specifically with drug abusers. She loved her job. It was a calling.

Her younger brother was an addict and she never got over when he overdosed at fifteen. Anyway, it was typical for the people at the rehab house, where she worked, to walk home in the evenings after the last group session. The place is on a dangerous road, Route 135."

She knew of it. Mostly because it had no sidewalks, no streetlights, and it was a common place for cops to nab speeders. The limit was 35 but everyone always did 55 or more.

O_2

Sydney studied Mark. She wondered why he mentioned Rt 135 and its dangers. He seemed to be lost in thought. The set of his shoulders and the way he held himself stiff. Ready to walk away if she said no to this. He would never leave Ryan alone. Either Ryan went or both stayed. And she needed Mark. Why did that need feel so strong? There were others with expertise in genetic engineering and CRISPR. Why did she want Mark to be on this team? She buried the thought. She felt her heart softening for that poor child who lost his mother when he was only nine. "Okay, Ryan can come but on one condition. Nothing interferes when we get to La Rinconada. Nothing."

CHAPTER
SIXTEEN

The day had been warm for December and the air was clear against the creamy white setting of the winter sun. It would be her last run at the Institute for a while. She changed into her sweats, laced her shoes, put on her old knit cap, and headed away from the office buildings. As she passed the window to her mother's office, she saw the lights go off. Her mother was heading home. Had the two ever been close. Ever played games? Her clouded memory filled with odd feelings of loss. Her footfalls slowed and became heavy on the gravel of the running path. When she needed someone to talk to, to help with this weight, she would call Aunt Rene. Dr. Rene DeSalvo was her mother's colleague at Mass General. Aunt Rene had often visited when Sydney was a young girl after grueling shifts with arms opened wide loaded down with special treats. Sydney never forgot Aunt Rene's kindness. She became a lifeline for a lonely girl. As the years passed, Dr. Rene DeSalvo became a world-renowned scientist for her specialties in evolutionary biology and microbiology. She had been recruited by a medical conglomerate and traveled most of the time. The last she had seen Aunt Rene was in New York five years ago.

They had dinner and the two discussed science and the work they were involved in. Sydney never questioned Aunt Rene about her past. Never thought about the friendship Aunt Rene had with her mother. There was no doubt she craved knowing more about her younger years and wanted to understand the unnatural coldness she always felt from her mother. But she didn't want to jeopardize the closeness with Aunt Rene. She welcomed the bits and pieces of memories that would intermittently come flooding into her consciousness when she least expected it. After that dinner she couldn't stop playing in her head an image of her younger self. Sydney had been in her room experimenting with a science set Aunt Rene had given her the day before for her seventh birthday. Her mother was in the kitchen talking on the phone. Sydney had crept toward the half-open bedroom door and held her breath as she listened to the conversation.

"I'm telling you; you're spoiling her. She doesn't need another *pink* microscope. She must learn to be a serious scientist, not playact at it." Her mother waited, listening. "Yes, yes, I know you love her, Rene. You have had an enormous impact on her life. I daresay she talks more about you than me most of the time." Her mother forced a laugh. "No, Rene, I'm not telling you to stop seeing her." Pause. "I know." Sydney felt her stomach cramp up and tears swelled in her eyes. Was her mother going to refuse to have Aunt Rene see her again? She couldn't imagine it. Her mother paced back and forth and then stopped at the sink turning on the faucet to fill a glass. She gently set it down. "You are the only person in the world that calms me down. You know me so well. I don't know what I would have done throughout these years without you in my life." Her mother picked up the glass again and took a sip. "I agree. You are good for Sydney too."

Sydney's father never had a role in her life. Her mother divorced him when she was an infant. He was a brilliant neuro-organ transplant physician. The last time she saw him he was the guest speaker at a graduate course conference. She went up to him afterwards. He knew who she was but treated her like another adoring fan. Even asked her if she wanted him to autograph her program.

As she grew older when Aunt Rene wasn't available, she dealt with her lack of a loving family by running through the streets of her neighborhood. The trees in the quiet suburban area and the steady beat of her feet on the sidewalk were her companions. No judgements. Running was something she had control over. No mother directing her life from afar. No absent father to mourn.

Steeling herself this last night before the journey to Peru, she pushed her legs to the limit. She welcomed the compelling urge to run until she collapsed.

CHAPTER
SEVENTEEN

. . . .

Sydney folded jeans, t-shirts, and her heavy sweater into a small canvas bag. Their flight was early the next morning. Yun's research on La Rinconada revealed temperatures in that part of Peru hovered at freezing year-round. Sydney made a mental note to remind Mark tonight to bring warm clothes and boots for Ryan. She would carry her parka and wear work boots. No fuss, no muss. "KISS - Keep it simple Syd" was how her friends from college jokingly described her. Her wardrobe consisted mainly of jeans and old brand name T's. Slogans such as "Coke, it's the REAL THING" and "Just Do It". At thirty-three she knew the Institute's younger staff had no idea what the slogans meant. For some reason she liked that. She did want her team to respect her, even like her but she also had a deep-seated need to remain apart from them. Never giving too much about who she was. She wondered sometimes what made her tick. Was she all about science like her mother or was she something more?

She ran through the list of last-minute tasks. The final round of inoculations was completed for herself and the staff. Darweshi arrived in La Rinconada last night. He hadn't been excited when he had learned he was the best candidate to head to Peru before everyone else.

He had recently returned five months ago from an expedition in Brazil and had most of the shots needed for another trip to South America. She had sent him to coordinate with the locals in La Rinconada and set up last minute items at the lab before they arrived.

She mentally checked off things on her list as she stuffed an OID into her bag along with a wrist monitor that measured internal oxygen levels. These OIDs or Oxygen Infusion Devices were small patches that provided, for the short-term, much-needed oxygen at that elevation. Each person on the team was required to have one. Replacing was necessary every twenty-four hours. She switched on her com-chip and flipped her VU monocle to the most recent hologram from Darweshi. Mark hated VU technology along with everything else techie. He called it the 'invasion monocle'. She grinned and hit play. The monocle displayed Darweshi's short round body slumped on a too-tiny chair for his frame in a peeling-brown wallpapered room with a twin bed and nightstand that held a lamp with horses painted on the shade. Darweshi got up and moved around as he talked.

"My feet are sore. Bring work boots not sneakers! My head hurts, and I'm dying for a cheeseburger from Leo's on Fulton." He took off his glasses and rubbed his eyes. "Anyway, it was tough getting here, you'll see. And when I arrived, I discovered two of the special refrigeration units were lost in transit," he shook his head. "I checked all the crates and thankfully there was no damage in any of the genetic holding equipment. The shipping company promised that the centrifuges and the replacement units will be here when you arrive, I'm keeping my fingers crossed." He stopped and looked out the small and only window in the room. He continued after a few seconds. "The people in the village stay to themselves. I talked a bit with the boarding house owner, Dario. He seems like a good guy, although not talkative. I tried to get friendly, swap some funny stories. Unfortunately, all I got was Katen Brothers run this whole town. But it all seems okay. Oh," he scratched the top of his head, "and this Art Saunders person, the Katen Brothers security guy, came to the warehouse and insisted I report to him at the end of each day." He rolled his eyes. "Anyway, this is Dar, signing off." He raised his hand in a salute. Then put his hands together in prayer, "One more thing, do you think you could bring me a burger?"

Sydney smiled at the last comment as she switched off the hologram and took off the VU monocle. She had expected the people there to be close-mouthed to newcomers. Especially since none of them knew why Darweshi was there. Dr. Davis had advised the local government in that part of Peru about the expedition, but only in high-level terms. Most of what they were doing there was highly confidential. But it was Darweshi's Art Saunders comment that nagged her. It wasn't the first time his name came up. During the initial review of La Rinconada, Mark discovered that there was no formal police force nor any type of authority, just Katen's special security officer, Art Saunders. She remembered Mark's comment the other day, something about being in the '1800's old west with one sheriff in town.'

Everything was ready. Early tomorrow morning Yun, Mark, and Ryan would meet her at the airport. Dr. Davis had secured the funding from the Institute's coffers and the necessary documents from the South American government and final approval from Wallace Katen. She found herself thankful that as the head of the Institute, her mother needed to remain in California and keep officials informed of the progress. The weight of the tasks ahead mounted as a physical force in her body, she didn't need her mother looking over her shoulder. And she refused to tell anyone about the reports that people may be dying from asphyxiation. She told herself it was circumstantial. There was too much at stake and her team was already under so much pressure.

CHAPTER
EIGHTEEN

• •

It was six p.m. the next day when they arrived in Cuzco, Peru. Nestled in the highlands of the Andes, Cuzco was one of the world's most beautiful cities. With Mark, Yun, and Sydney in back and Ryan, who insisted, in the front seat, they had packed into the tiny cab, and headed to the hotel, Palacio del Inka. The turquoise sky blended with the red ochre mountains. Sydney gazed out the side window absorbing the colorful ponchos and black felt hats and smiled as the people laughed and gathered in the squares. The sun blazed down and pulsated against the walls of the buildings. Sydney felt the energy surging inside of her.

The taxi driver talked non-stop about Cuzco and its rich history. "Palacio del Inka dates back to the 15th century and stands on land that was once the Incan palace of the Sun," he said with a lyrical accent. He glanced to the back seat through the mirror and was nodding his head to emphasize the beauty that came into view. "The city had been designed in the shape of a puma." He took both hands off the wheel and used them to shape what was supposed to be a puma. The taxi lurched to one side, just missing a parked car. Sydney, sitting between Mark and Yun, grabbed Mark's thigh to keep herself from crashing into him. He looked down at her hand.

She yanked it away and turned, hiding her warm face. To alleviate her reaction and give herself time to recover, she spoke louder than necessary filling the cab, "No wonder there's incredible art here." She awkwardly spread her arms toward the side window. "There's so much inspiration." She wanted to sound calm but wasn't sure she pulled it off.

The taxi stopped, and the driver swiveled in his seat. "We are here."

Sydney anxious to get out pushed Yun out the door and stepped up into the lobby. Enthralled by the colors of the buildings' walls, mirroring the red and gold of the mountains she forgot her uneasiness and soaked up the beauty. Palace of the sun. A better name couldn't've been found. The art occupying every space on the walls was breathtaking, filled with warrior angels and wild cats. Pumas were a popular theme.

After check-in, Yun ran ahead with Ryan to the elevators, leaving Mark walking beside Sydney.

"Want to meet at the hotel restaurant?" he said. "I'd like to get something to eat. Airline food just doesn't do it for me." The four stepped into the elevator.

Mark hit the buttons for their floors. Sydney felt drained from the flight. She saw her reflection in the elevator as the doors closed. Her hair was flat and dirty against her head and her body was tense anticipating the tasks ahead. But she was famished. "I could go for something. I'll shower first and head down."

Mark's face brightened. "Great. Ryan and I will get settled."

Yun patted his stomach. "I stuffed myself with chips, peanuts, and protein bars so I'm not hungry. I was going to teach Ryan how to play this game I brought."

"I'm not hungry either, Dad," Ryan whispered. "I want to learn the game."

Sydney considered whether she should have dinner with him. But when the elevator arrived at her floor, she turned to Mark, "It may take me an hour. I need to make a few calls. Let's meet in the restaurant about eight." She hadn't eaten since early morning as her stomach kept reminding her. That was the only reason.

In her room, she grabbed a favorite navy V-neck shirt and beige cotton pants from the suitcase. She jumped in the shower and twenty minutes later she logged onto her computer and reviewed tomorrow's schedule. It included an early train to Puno, Peru. Once in Puno, the final leg of the trip was a mountainous drive up to La Rinconada. She placed a call. "Buenos noches señor. Do you speak English? Oh, good… my name is Sydney Davis. I requested transportation to La Rinconada from Puno train station. I'm confirming."

The man told her that after arriving in Puno they were to wait at the train station for a local van that would take them up the mountain. The driver would be holding a sign that said "La Rinconada". As Sydney disconnected the call, she shook her head. The man mentioned the ride up to La Rinconada could be *uneasy*. Maybe she had misinterpreted his English.

She rubbed the back of her neck trying to relieve the strain she felt building again. She had one more call to make – mother. Her mother would be at the office anticipating the daily status call. She sighed. The call would take less than ten minutes but, as always, the anxiety built up beforehand, making it much worse. She hated having to report every detail and be grilled about every decision.

Sydney went into the bathroom. She fussed with her hair, finally settling on letting the bangs cover part of her eye in a careful yet still careless way. She applied a bit of mascara and a soft pink lipstick. As she studied her face in the mirror, she convinced herself that tonight would be about a beautiful city and enjoying dinner. She turned and left the room fully knowing that she didn't call her mother. Not tonight. She couldn't deal with her tonight. With a mind open to possibilities and hope for a better future for the world, she relaxed and took the stairs to the lobby.

She arrived a few minutes early and wandered around finally stopping at the restaurant. A painting at the entrance piqued her interest. It depicted a woman holding a child, Madonna-like. The title was Virgin of Pomato, in glorious gold leaf and colors of the mountains, rich red ochre and multiple shades of green. All these colors seemed to direct her to an uncommon shade of blue eyes in the portrait.

The hostess approached and smiled. "Do you like it, senorita?"

"Yes, very much." Sydney said. "Is it another Andean deity?"

The hostess nodded. "Our earth goddess, Pachamama. She protects the earth and all its living things."

Sydney suddenly felt a chill, almost a foreboding. She backed up from the painting. Would their plan at La Rinconada work? What if it didn't? She hoped Pachamama was as powerful as her believers seemed to think.

"Senorita? Uh, Miss? Are you bien?"

Shaking herself, she nodded her head vigorously. "I'm fine, fine. Thank you." She blinked and gave a half-smile. "I'll need a table for two."

The hostess guided her to a small table near the windows overlooking the mountains she'd seen in the painting. Across the room a couple sat with their heads close, almost touching, their hands entwined. The moon cast a romantic glow on their faces. She yearned for that kind of closeness and hoped one day she would feel it again. She pulled her eyes away from the couple. Even in the face of imminent extinction, it would seem she still had a desire for connection, for love. Sydney pulled notes from her bag, attempting to bring herself back to reality.

"Hey." Mark dropped in the chair next to her. He nodded toward the papers she clenched. "How about we enjoy this beautiful place tonight. We'll have enough of that when we get to La Rinconada."

"Sorry, I didn't see you arrive." She avoided his concerned stare and shoved the documents back in her bag. "So, Yun and Ryan? I would never put them together as friends. I thought Ryan didn't speak to people?" She hoped to keep the conversation off her.

Mark shrugged. "Somehow Yun finds ways to communicate with him. They've gotten close during this trip. Ryan is calm with Yun."

Sydney tried to study the menu, but his hands were on the table close to hers. Large with long fingers. Strong hands. Hands that weren't afraid to reach out.

"Would you like a glass of wine?" His voice was low almost a whisper.

She snapped out of her daze. Mark's green eyes softened. His arms flexed and he leaned in. He appeared to be waiting for something. To hear some word from her. He'd been part of her team for two years. She admitted to herself that she wanted the physical intensity, the closeness she remembered, after all she was human. She wanted what the couple across the room had. She longed for the distraction, the feeling of being just two in a world of billions, even if just for few hours. Maybe this was it. Once they got to La Rinconada no one could predict what was going to happen. Yet, the drama of how she walked out on him years ago held her back. She had never given him an explanation. One that he could understand.

Mark drummed his fingers on the table. She placed a hand over his. His hand stilled and was warm beneath her cool one. Light from the candles shone across his face. He moved closer.

So close his lips touched her hair, "I still care for you."

She felt his other hand cover hers. The flutter in her belly had nothing to do with being hungry. She drew her hand back and stared at the white tablecloth. "I'm sorry."

Finally. She said the words she'd been meaning to say for way too long.

"Sorry?" He looked confused.

"For how I left you." There, it was out. She shifted in her chair and her knee brushed against him. Her hand was still so close to his. She relaxed this time when he reached over lacing his fingers into hers.

"Sydney, it's okay. Please look at me. It's okay." A smile broke across his face as her eyes lifted. A full minute passed as she processed what to do next, what to say. Mark dragged his chair closer interrupting her jumbled thoughts. "So how about that wine?"

She got a whiff of his scent that ignited memories from years ago. Goosebumps tingled along her thigh.

The waitress appeared from nowhere and filled their glasses with water. "Can I get you something to drink?"

Without taking his eyes from Sydney he addressed the waitress, "We'll have a bottle of the cabernet, the one that is featured today on your wine list."

"Excellent." The waitress seemed to hide a smile as she spun around.

"So, guess I'll have a glass." She took a deep breath and exhaled slowly. The corners of her mouth lifted into a forced smile as she unlocked her hand from his and slid it back to her side of the table.

"Syd, can we talk? About what happened? You know, back then at Harvard." She could hear her blood pumping through her body. She knew she needed this but struggled with protecting them both from a long-buried memory. His memory of her in college was so far from who she was now. She looked at the table and brushed imaginary crumbs from the white cloth. "I've changed since college. I'm not the same."

He tilted his head to the side, "People don't change that much. I always felt we had something very special. I almost went crazy when your mother ordered you to go work for the Institute. You still had so much you planned to do before she put you on that path." His brow furrowed. "The same path as hers by the way." He grabbed the water glass and held it. His voice faded to a whisper, "Why did you do it?".

Sydney felt an emptiness with those words. Words that she ran over and over in her head. Why? She had wanted to stay with Mark and continue her research at the college. She had never explained fully to him how torn she was back then. Her mother's reasons gave her an excuse to leave. She regretted never explaining things to him. Now it was too late. Too late for explanations, too late for everything. Several years later when Sydney heard that Mark had married Catherine it solidified her decision. She forced herself to forget the life she'd dreamed of and settled into a routine at the Institute.

"I don't know why." The lie felt bitter on her tongue as it echoed in her head.

The waitress returned, set the wine glasses on the table, and opened the bottle with a flourish. She poured the wine into Mark's glass and waited. He sipped it and nodded. As she filled Sydney's glass she said, "The specialty of the restaurant is roast guinea pig with orange sauce and rice. Would you like to try it?"

They remained quiet. She needed a better ending than what she left him with all those years ago. Afterall there is only now. And now was pretty scary. The world could be a totally different place tomorrow. She needed this connection even if it was fleeting. Brushing her leg against Mark's thigh she said to the waitress. "I think perhaps we're both too tired for food." She waited to gauge Mark's reaction. His eyes opened wide then softened. Taking this as a yes, she said to the waitress before she could regret it, "We've changed our minds. I'm sorry, please charge the wine to Room 328."

The waitress looked from Mark to Sydney, "Si. Si, of course." She quietly moved from the table.

Sydney wondered if this was fair to him. But the reaction where their bodies touched created a fire under her skin that made her feel like she'd explode. They were in a place surrounded by amazing beauty and before she realized what was happening his hand drew her up from the chair. Feeling like she was in a movie she searched his face and said, "How about we see if there is something in the room refrigerator and have a drink in my room? Let these few hours be. . . just us."

In the elevator they remained close to each other, whispering in each other's ear, laughing at a shared joke. She didn't want this feeling to dissolve. He held her hand and rubbed his thumb against her palm on the way up. There had been no one special in her life since him.

No one that could create this tingling and heady rush.

When they got there, she fumbled to find her key and unlocked the door, all the time feeling his presence directly behind her. His breath made the hairs on the back of her neck prickle. Before pushing the door open, she turned around. The chemistry between them flooded into her. She stood there for a moment then pulled herself up on her toes and leaned into him. He dropped his head and with a softness that unleashed every memory, he kissed her. She felt his hands caress the back of her neck pulling her closer for something deeper. They were back in that college apartment. It was as if they had never parted. A moment later they were inside the room. She heard the door click closed. He backed her up until her legs hit the bed. They toppled onto the mattress and sunk into its softness. Moments later she let go of all the anxiety of the present, all the darkness in her past.

CHAPTER
NINETEEN

December 19, 2039

La Rinconada, Peru

h-ODD 168
Oxygen level 20.4

During the ride up the mountain to La Rinconada Sydney was sure they would be vaulted to their death. There were more twists and turns than she could count, and all while climbing at a 30-degree angle. She risked a glance at her companions. Ryan and Yun seemed to be fine, and Mark, busy studying his notes, appeared unflustered. Was he thinking about what happened last night at all? Did he have regrets? Her hand was frozen in a lock-grip on the door handle. Would she ever be able to conquer her fears? She tried focusing on the windshield and even resorted to closing her eyes when it became unbearable. Her forehead held beads of sweat and they trickled down randomly stinging her eyes. She risked rubbing her hand on the burning closed lids and opening them just as the driver careened around a dangerous switchback. A blinding mass of blue ice atop a barren mountain magically appeared. A magnificent remnant left by the ice age millions of years ago. This must be La Bella Durmiente, the Sleeping Beauty glacier. Its presence was dominating and forceful. They were at the top of the Andes.

Darweshi sprinted toward the van as soon as it stopped. "You're finally here!" Sydney struggled to get her body moving again and onto solid ground. The rest of the team piled out of the truck and seemed no worse for the wear from a ride that had relentlessly banged them forty miles straight up the mountain. Sydney turned in a full circle, taking in her first look at La Rinconada. But it wasn't the view that made her stop short.

"What's that smell?' She tried holding her breath then finally released it only to take in even more of the hideous odor.

Dar came into view as she was trying to pinch her nostrils closed. "I forgot to tell you about it."

She looked at him over her knuckles. "Forgot to tell me?", her voice vibrated in her head. Sydney knew all too well what that vibrating meant. Hopefully the migraine wouldn't last its usual twenty-four hours.

"Uh, yeah. The garbage. And the lack of sewers. You'll get used to it." He paused to point toward the glacier, "Then there's the gold mine. Lots of runoff of sulfuric acid. I think that's what it is. It could be adding to the smell and it seeps into the tundra. This place is an environmental disaster.

The smoke coming from pipes atop numerous squat buildings mixed with the cloudy sky cast an eerie yellowish glow around the base of the misted glacier. The van had stopped right before a sign made of animal skins with words scratched in black paint. One side hung lopsided across two ten-foot poles welcoming visitors – BIENVENIDOS a RINCONADA. As she came back around and faced Darweshi, he grabbed her in a bear hug, knocking the breath out of her. "I have a lot to tell you."

He stepped back and waved to everyone else. Sydney, still reeling from the final leg of the journey and coping with a stink that heightened the painful throbbing in her head, didn't fail to notice Darweshi's edginess. He took his glasses on and off, supposedly cleaning them, a nervous habit. They had only been out of touch for less than two days. What was bothering him?

Mark had looked like a giant spring uncoiling as he climbed out from the backseat. He'd rubbed the thick muscles in his neck and stretched his long legs. Seeing him move like that reminded her of their few hours in her hotel room. He'd been so much taller than the bed was long. And so much stronger than she'd remembered. The thought made her trip as her legs buckled. She steadied herself before anyone noticed. She glanced back at her team. Mark was busy whispering something to Ryan. Yun seemed to be absorbed by the unusual surroundings.

On several occasions during the journey Sydney considered Mark's insistence to take Ryan along. Ryan had a few uncomfortable episodes right at the start of the trip. Getting on the flight out of California, Ryan plastered himself against Mark. He refused to go any further. Sydney felt compassion. It was not an easy one for a child, especially one with ASD. Then Yun had surprised her, when on the plane ride from California he took an interest in Ryan and taught him the game he brought along. Ryan stayed content, mesmerized by the tactics and graphic patterns. She eavesdropped as Yun talked non-stop about his older brother, Chin, who taught him about gaming when Yun was about the same age as Ryan. She could swear that Yun was just a boy too, especially when he played the game, his body bobbed up and down. When he had mentioned his brother Chin she recalled how pain, or maybe it was sadness, clouded his features. She determined to find out more once she had a spare minute.

"So, this is La Rinconada," Mark slowly turned in a circle taking it all in. "Looks like it hasn't been touched by the outside world in hundreds of years."

"And we like it that way," said a gravelly voice from behind them.

They all spun toward the sound. A bear of a man with a bald head and a snake tattoo wrapped around his neck stood in the spot the van just vacated.

"This is Art Saunders," Darweshi said. "He's in charge of security."

"Much more than security." Art strode toward Sydney. "I run the whole damn show here on the mountain." He stopped a foot in front of her. "You must be the gal they told me about. You're the one who heads this team of . . . scientists?"

Was that sarcastic? That drawl reminded her of some distant relatives she had in Texas. Sydney held out her hand and waited for him to take it. After an uncomfortable few seconds, he reluctantly took her hand and yanked her arm up and down. His hand was hard and calloused. This guy might test her already depleted patience. "Nice to meet you, Mr. Saunders. You already met Darweshi. Let me introduce you to the rest of the team. This is Mar..."

"What the hell are two boys doin' here? Nobody told me about any kids coming." Art interrupted, looking beyond Mark at Ryan and Yun.

"It's one boy and it's none of your business." Mark glared and his jaw tightened.

Art turned his stare at Yun who had his chin pointed out. He pulled his hair off his face and stared straight back at the bulky man. "I'm eighteen!"

Mark advanced toward Art while Yun simmered. Sydney finally found her voice. "We're all exhausted." She stepped in between Art and Mark. "Let's get some rest, meet officially tomorrow. Then we'll go over any specific requirements and talk about the work we're doing. I appreciate your stopping to welcome us." She directed Darweshi. "Dar, please help with the bags and drive us to our rooms. Now."

Art kicked up a bit of dirt. "I'll be waiting for you in my office right over there," he pointed to a run-down shack, "at seven a.m. sharp." He turned and walked to the wooden shack slamming the door behind him.

Driving on the main dusty road of the town in a pre-2000 Subaru, which he borrowed from the owners of the boarding house, Darweshi talked nonstop about the food and the lack of activity. "Just about everyone in the settlement works in the mines during the day. There are some kids but they're only around after school. It's like a social desert here." Darweshi craved social contact. But Sydney knew him well enough to see that something else was bothering him.

He was fidgety, waving his arms back and forth as he drove.

As he continued to talk about how food was trucked in each day, Sydney took in the surroundings. In the distance the homes were perched on the side of a slope. They were either grey metal that looked like it was peeled back with ribbed tin roofs, or old brick structures with stove pipe funnels pumping out along the sides. Smoke billowed everywhere. Broken sections of concrete forced the car to pitch up, down, and sideways. Her backside was getting sore. And oh, how her head ached. She distracted herself from the pain by concentrating of where she was. Along the side of the road, she swore were pieces of bones that created a ghost-like fossilized scene. Men and women walked up the steep paths of the mountain that most likely led to the mine. There were hand-painted statues of a woman next to some of the houses. She recognized the likeness of Pachamama from the painting in the hotel. She could hear a distant sound of clanking from the gold mining machinery. The sullen drudgery permeated everywhere. The long travel day had begun at five a.m. in Cuzco, and finally by nine p.m. the team arrived at the one boarding house in La Rinconada. Darweshi and Yun roomed together. Mark and Ryan were down the hall next to the common bathroom and Sydney had her own room with a bath. Darweshi introduced them to Dario and Azucena, owners of the establishment. Both were friendly and Sydney thanked them for allowing Dar to use their vehicle. Azucena offered them something to eat but Sydney declined. Azucena was holding her very large belly as she spoke to them. She was pregnant. Sydney surmised she was close to her due date. She wondered what medical facilities were available in this remote place.

"I'll just take my key please," Sydney said. She needed a place to think and be alone.

"There are no keys, senorita. There is no need." Azucena held up her palms as if to say we have no need for locks here.

Sydney nodded but didn't understand. How can they not have keys? She headed to her room, without a thought as to what the rest of the team did. Her room held one wooden chair against the wall near the tiny window, one small bed, no bureau. It was cold, but she didn't really care. Ready to collapse, she sat on the bed, peeled off her boots and rubbed her feet with her coat still on. Over the spitting noise of the heater, she heard shuffling footsteps in the hallway that stopped outside her door. Then a soft knock.

"Syd……Sydney?"

It was Darweshi. She lifted herself from the bed and spoke through the door. "I'm exhausted. Can it wait till morning?"

"Open up. Please!"

She was surprised at his insistence. As soon as the door opened, he pushed past her. "This Art guy is no good."

Sydney shut the door and squeezed her temple with her fingers. She felt her head throb. "Do you have something tangible you want to tell me or is this going to be a discussion of a personality clash with the security officer?" She was irritable. Upset. Tired. She dropped down on the only chair in the room. Darweshi had a history of disliking people before he even knew them. Well, maybe, it wasn't that he disliked someone. If she was honest, he was just like her. It was a trust issue. Whenever she met someone new it would be many conversations later before she would trust – even then she would never totally open up. Trust was a dear thing in her world, and she didn't give it up lightly.

"He's no good!" Dar blurted out. She started to shake her head then Darweshi held up a hand, "Okay, okay, just let me get this out. Over the past two days I've seen some strange goings-on late at night." Without invitation he planted himself on the edge of the bed. He looked at her and waited a second, "I was having a hard time sleeping, so I'd go out for walks. One night I see Art moving crates about three a.m. into this old beat-up jeep from one of the crumbling warehouses that he told me was empty. He's all quiet-like, sneaking around, looking back and forth, like he doesn't want anyone seeing him." Darweshi shook his head, "Along with his crappy attitude when I got here and his freaky insistence to let him know whenever I left the lab during the day, it got me wondering."

"Those crates could be food supplies, or medical equipment, or a host of other things." Sydney yawned. She couldn't understand why Darweshi was so upset, almost frightened. "I know," he breathed in sounding unconvinced, "But on the second night he's with Dario. He's yelling, angry, and waving that ridiculous security stick he carries everywhere. Almost smacking him when the poor guy dropped one of the containers he was moving. I almost took off when I saw that. But I couldn't move. I kept thinking 'what's he's doing that for if it's just supplies?' I don't know. I just don't trust him. From what I could see, all Dario did was drop one of the crates and a liquid substance spilled onto the floor of the warehouse. That's the stuff seeping into the ground here. The runoff from the mine. Ugh!" He shook his head, "Dario had a mask on. I'm going to figure out what he's using sulfuric acid for. Something just doesn't feel right."

"Yes, good idea." Sydney rubbed her temples. She was exhausted and couldn't stifle another yawn but knew the pain of her migraine was going to keep her awake.

Darweshi watched her. Sydney could tell he wanted to talk more. "I see you're not feeling well, Syd. You know I'll do anything for you. I noticed how shaken you were when you got off that van today. Please tell me what I can do. That ride would scare most people".

"Oh, well, yeah, I was shaken. I don't do well with heights. Not sure if I ever told you about that part of me."

"You never *explicitly* told me. But I sorta have known for a while now." Dar went to the bathroom and grabbed the cup on the sink and filled it with water. He came back out. "Here, drink some water. You need hydration. I also brought some ibuprofen." He reached in his pocket and took out the capsules.

"Thanks, Dar." She threw the pills into her mouth and sipped the water. "You're a good friend."

"Do you think you can sleep? I can go. Just want to make sure you're okay."

"Actually, I don't think I can sleep quite yet. Why don't you stay?" She considered how much time the two of them spent together working and how little they really knew about each other's lives. Maybe it's time to trust someone. "There's a story I'd like to tell you. Maybe talking about it will be a first step in getting over this crazy fear of heights."

Darweshi settled comfortably back on the edge of the bed. He waited.

Sydney placed her hands in her lap and looked out into the distance, "I was five. Our house was a three story Victorian with several roof levels. My bedroom was on the third floor. Mother wanted to make sure I became independent at an early age. She didn't want me too close to where she slept so it wouldn't be easy to sneak into her room if I got scared or something bothered me." She snuck a look at Dar. She never talked to anyone about her mother's way of raising her.

Dar's dropped his head. "Geez!" He looked back up and nodded encouraging her to go on.

"Because of the distance between us, I would find ways to occupy myself. I'd make up games with an imaginary friend. A few times I climbed on the flat roof that was right outside my bedroom window. I sat there for hours. Mother finally caught me one day. She forbad me to ever go out on the roof again. Then turned away as if that was all the energy she'd waste on the subject. She simply expected me to obey." Sydney let out a long sigh. "I was so young then and confused. She never gave me any attention. The next day after she told me not to go out there, I did. She knew I was there. Next thing she was in my room slammed the window shut and walked out. I ran to the window and tried to open it. But an old Victorian house with old Victorian windows?" She shrugged. "I couldn't manage. Didn't have the strength. I banged on the glass and screamed for her. I waited. Then I heard her car pull out of the driveway. I forgot where I was and ran to the edge of the roof." She heard Dar gasp. She went over to him and placed a hand on his hand. "I didn't fall off but I was terrified. She left me out there for hours. It was twilight when she finally came home and opened the window."

"I'm so sorry, Syd." He stood and hugged her.

She hugged him back. Her head wasn't throbbing anymore.

CHAPTER
TWENTY

• •

The day that Yun had heard about the death of his brother Chin, he was at a local bar with his friends in Sacramento celebrating his acceptance into Stanford.

A businessman had been seated at the next table talking to his companion about an explosion on the Chinese/Russian border. Yun had been half listening until he heard him say 'ecoterrorists'. He had heard through some of Chin's old friends that his brother was involved in an organization called *Seeds of Tomorrow* whose mission was to bomb any traitors to the environment. Last he had heard, Chin was somewhere in northern China.

Yun had never told anyone what had transpired between him and his brother that final day. No one, not even his parents knew that Chin had joined a radical group. They had just accepted Chin's absence as part of his need for adventure. They told friends that their son Chin was a wanderer and that the small village they lived in was never enough. Yun surmised they were secretly happy he was gone. They didn't have enough money for the two boys and having one gone was easily accepted.

Yun had never given up that one day he would see his brother again. He had realized all his achievements were attributed to his deep-seated desire to impress his brother. He had wanted his brother to be proud of him.

Yun approached the businessman at the next table.

"Excuse me, did you say that there was an explosion on the Chinese/Russian border this morning?"

The man sipped his drink and eyed Yun. "Yeah. A bunch of crazy ecoterrorists bombed the railroad crossing between China and Russia. They claimed it was to bring attention to the continued use of fossil fuel that gets transported via the railroad. A lot of people were killed."

"Did they say what group was responsible?"

"I think it was 'Tomorrow something' or 'Sons of Tomorrow'? Not sure. They said all the terrorists died in the explosion."

Yun's drink had slipped out of his hand, crashing to the floor.

Sometime during his last year at Stanford, a man had approached Yun. He said he knew his brother Chin. Without truly understanding what he was getting involved in, Yun had the why. He was intent on seeking vindication for his brother's death. Everything from now on would be dedicated to Chin's memory and Chin's mission - whatever that involved.

CHAPTER
TWENTY-ONE

S ydney felt cautious about the seven-a.m. meeting. The morning accentuated her feeling by being cloudy and cold, a repeat of yesterday. The ever-present glacier seemed to hold the village in an invisible grasp. She walked watching her footing over the rocks and ice to Art's office holding a scarf against her nose to block the smell that never let up. Dar said she'd get used to it.

Sydney shook off her morning malaise leftover from the emotional talk with Dar last night. She hoped the meeting this morning would go well. Along with the emotions dug up from her past she also had to deal with Darweshis' fears last night of what he saw Art doing. She was able to convince him to concentrate on the project goals and CRISPR edits. Her worries, however, were not so easily allayed. She knocked and stepped up into the wooden box of an office. Not more than ten by ten. Art and Mark were already there. She figured Mark would show up after that reception from Art. Mark greeted her and stood when she entered. Art fussed with papers sitting at a desk that took up most of the space.

"Good morning. Thanks for coming. So, the rules around here are, first," Art began, "I check up on your status at random times during the day." He cleared his throat and added as an afterthought, "to make sure you don't need anything."

She stood next to Mark and felt his shift from one foot to another. They both remained silent.

"Second, the mountain paths are off limits. Only the locals are allowed and then only the ones who work in the mines or have business with the mine."

Mark moved closer to Art's desk, "We are here to just do a job and then we'll be gone. I understand your need to keep people off the mountain. We have no need to go anywhere near there." Sydney made a mental note to speak with Mark about what Darweshi told her last night. But she decided it had nothing to do with them. Everybody has secrets and her team cannot get involved in anything but what they came here to do.

Art leaned back in his chair and puffed out his chest. She had dealt with people like him.

Control was their normal way of life. One person came to mind.

Dar had done some quick research last night and this sulfuric acid had dangerous longterm effects. She decided to poke the bear. "I see many people wearing masks around here. Is there something poisonous we should know about?"

"What?" Art shuffled some papers on his desk. "No need for you to concern yourself.

We are following all the OSHA guidelines and there is nothing for you to worry about."

Mark gave her a quizzical look that said, 'something else we need to talk about?'. He turned and spoke to Art, "Fine. We will stay away from your mine and we'll take your word about following all the government guidelines."

"Yeah, well that's good. Cuz there's some wild pumas in these mountains. I don't wanna be responsible for any accidents." He stressed the last word.

Yun had not mentioned the wild pumas when he delivered his report of La Rinconada.

"Is there anything else?" Mark waited, folding his arms across his chest.

Art lifted his head. From her angle, she got a good look at the inked snake coiled around his neck. It looked evil with the fangs ready to attack. She also noticed the corner of the patch that infused oxygen into his blood. "Not right now. I'll let you know." At that Mark tilted forward.

Sydney stepped in front of Mark facing him. "We need to get to the lab. Everyone is waiting for us." Mark didn't move. She ended up grabbing Mark's hand and dragging him out the door.

Sydney and Mark walked through the main part of town. Most of the locals were already working at the mines and those who were not, stayed inside their small houses with the pipes from the roofs blowing smoke from the warming fires. The air was thick with fog and the day a depressing scene from a second-rate movie. The debris strewn along the side of the road were scraps of skeleton bones, her initial thought yesterday. She bent down to look closer. The bones were from mammals, medium-sized. She stood to ask Mark about them but he strode by her making his way to the lab. She yelled out to his back, "Dar came to see me last night."

Mark stopped walking to face her. "What for?"

"Everything's alright. It's just," she waited to finish as she caught up, "he saw Art late one night before we all arrived moving containers in one of the remote warehouses behind the mine. He said Dario and some other locals were helping him and Art got angry when one of the containers spilled."

Mark clenched his fist open and closed. She knew him as a clear-headed thinker, he never jumped to conclusions. "Art rubs me the wrong way. I have a feeling there's something he's hiding. Especially after he told us not to go on the mine paths. If you want, I can talk to Darweshi and investigate this."

"I thought about looking into him. But for now, let's keep it on the back burner. I can't spare a minute on anything but the gene edit. We have way too much going on. Our only priority is the gene edit. The oxygen levels are holding at 20.4%."

"I've already identified the gene to modify. So, for the next few days Yun and I will design the customized RNA guide to target the DNA. The last step is to build a template for the repair and build it into the CRISPR complex. This is when we need to gather samples of the

DNA from the locals." He stopped and grabbed her arm, "You did get permission for us to request their DNA?"

"Dr. Davis laid the groundwork. I was told we need to talk to the local medical doctor here. He's their spiritual leader too."

TWENTY-TWO

The first two days passed, without any incident and Art faded into the background. The team got into a routine and Sydney closely monitored all aspects of the plan. Back in California Mark had already established the gene they would cut. Now they worked on designing the custom guide and the delicate process of inserting it into a cell that would be the vehicle for CRISPR. Each day was a step toward completion. A solution for humankind. Each wore their wrist monitors that reported oxygen levels being infused into their bodies. The patch was against the skin on their chests; it's what kept them alive at this altitude and another reminder of where they were and what they were working on. Ryan appeared to take it all in stride walking to the lab in the morning with Mark, but sometimes Yun volunteered to take him and Mark allowed it. Mark was slowly letting Ryan expand his social boundaries. After the information Dar shared regarding the sulfuric acid, Mark made sure Ryan had a mask on as well as his OID. This was not a very safe place. Maybe he should have listened to Sydney and not taken his son. Darweshi had settled down and was no longer on edge with what he saw at the abandoned warehouse that night. He got into a daily routine and kept busy with the project. He enjoyed making snacks for Ryan in the afternoon and read climatology reports in the evening, keeping Sydney updated on the status of oxygen levels around the globe. Yun played his game in the evening and no one wandered off toward the mine paths. Yet, Sydney was tense. She couldn't shake her unease about what was at stake. The absoluteness of what they were doing. It was difficult enough to concentrate with an unburdened mind but what had happened with Mark in Cuzco randomly invaded her thoughts. At night, right before she closed her eyes, she'd feel the remembered warmth of Mark's body and would turn toward that dreamy vision as sleep enveloped her. She got angry thinking of how a little thing like sex jumbled her thoughts.

On the third full day there, Sydney arrived at the lab before dawn. Mark was already at his station.

He got off his stool. "Want some coffee? I just made a fresh batch." She circled around him and went directly to her small office. She sat down and began tapping on her computer.

"Syd?"

"What?" She kept her head down jamming one of the keys. She had almost forgotten after that night in Cuzco that she'd promised to let nothing distract her.

"We need to discuss what happened in Cuzco."

Sydney didn't look up.

"Syd? We can't ignore this."

Sydney held herself rigid. She knew he was right, but this was far from the best time.

"This isn't going away. I'm not going away." Mark's voice raised a notch. More insistent.

Sydney picked up her head and quickly scanned the lab. No one else had arrived yet. "I'm sorry but Dr. Davis wants me to finish this review of the process for rebuilding with blueprint DNA today."

Mark walked over to her and placed his palms on her desk. "Your mother can wait. Look at me."

Sydney pushed out of her chair. She felt her face turn hot. She threw up her hands and walked across the lab. "What I'm doing now, what we're doing now, is critical. Please don't do this."

Mark had been moving around her desk as she had started talking but then stopped when she pushed past him to the opposite side of the room. He called out to her back, "I'm not going to stop. We need to talk about what happened between us. You and I were in love once.

You should at least honor what we had."

Just then Darweshi hurried in the door rubbing and blowing on his hands. "Doesn't this place get any other weather besides cold and dreary?" He gave them a quizzical glance, then looked away and went to his station.

Sydney winced. She knew Darweshi heard something. Mark had a booming voice when he wanted to be heard.

A few minutes later Yun rushed in with Ryan, "Was this place the only option for our lab?" He directed the question at Darweshi.

"This was the only location shown to me. Art never mentioned any other options," Darweshi said as he removed drawers from the refrigeration units and placed them on the table.

Laid out in rows on trays were the guide sequences for the CRISPR injections. They had designed several and now had several iterations of the one that would be used to specifically target the DNA structure. These were precious.

"It's isolated. It's a hike to get here." Yun sounded angry. He brought Ryan over to the half-finished jigsaw puzzle that was in the small side room they used for lunch.

"What's with you?" Darweshi called to Yun and threw up his hands. "Is this weather making everyone miserable?" Darweshi went to yank out another tray.

"Careful!" Sydney yelled out.

Yun walked back in the lab and went over to Darweshi, "I just don't like how this old, unstable building sits against the side of the mountain. Those loose rocks and gravel can be dangerous with the steep slope. There's no vegetation to hold the rock back." Tempers simmered. The stress of the monumental task ahead of them was weighing on the whole team.

Ryan appeared to be the only one not looking for a fight today.

Sydney stopped in front of Yun. "We all need to get to work." She supposed living in California could give anyone a scare about landslides. She certainly didn't need something else to worry about or have them going off on tangents when they had to stay focused. "Today we must complete the initial blueprint genome. If not, we fall behind the deadline. Yun, I'll require those blueprint samples by tonight." The final step for the CRISPR cocktail was to add the template for the repair process. This was the blueprint DNA.

Yun had attempted to collect DNA from the local villagers. He had reported that some of the locals refused to give DNA samples. Sydney had gone searching for the medical doctor who she hoped would help them with the samples. She asked Dario who he was. The answer was vague and she couldn't pin down where this man lived. So, she cajoled a few of the people she met in the town to provide samples but she knew the tests required backups in case something went wrong. A few were not enough. She didn't want to bother Azucena who was so late into her pregnancy but there was no time left. She would talk to her tonight. It seemed every step forward came with two back. These people were the key. Everything depended on getting the samples. If not then all of this was for nothing.

Around lunchtime Mark stretched and stood up from his lab station, "Ryan." After a few seconds he looked around. "Ryan?" He stopped at Yun's station, "Where did you leave Ryan when you came in?"

Yun got up and peeked into the lunchroom and gazed toward the empty chair where he had left Ryan. "Right here, at the jigsaw." Mark followed behind Yun.

"He's not here!"

"Did you check the bathroom?" Sydney called out.

Mark hustled to the bathroom door, knocked once, and opened it, "Ryan?" He spun around. "He's not there!" He searched under the lab tables, behind the counters, and finally looking out the windows. "Ryan!" He shouted.

"Calm down. I'm sure he's not far." Sydney felt her heart race and a strong pull inside her stomach. "We'll find him." She grabbed her coat and barely stepped outside when Mark almost knocked her down and ran around the building, "Ryan! Ryan!"

Mark came back to the front of the building. He stopped short before colliding with Art. "Where's Ryan?" Mark's voice quaked. He seemed to be losing control. His tall muscular build blocked Art's short but stockier one from taking another step.

"I've no idea what you're talking about!" Art looked past Mark toward Sydney. "What's goin' on here?" He stepped around Mark. "What's he shout'n about?"

"Mark's son, Ryan, wandered off," Sydney said watching Mark as he bounded up the mountainside path to the mines, yelling Ryan's name.

"Hey, he can't go up there! Hey, you, get back here!" Art chased him up the path.

"Hoy boy, this isn't good," Darweshi stepped out of the doorway following Yun. "Dar, stay here in case Ryan returns," Sydney said. "Yun, you go to the boarding house and see if he's there. He may have gone back for some reason."

She scampered up the gravel path, slipping a few times. She let out a loud huff as she almost crashed into Art's back. When she recovered her balance, there in front of her, was an old man who held Ryan's hand.

Mark was on his knees in front of Ryan. The old man was with them on the edge of a crystal-clear pool that sparkled in the sun. Mark whispered to Ryan who nodded making his light brown curls bounce and looked up at the old man who held his hand. Mark stood. The man was a head shorter than Sydney. A menagerie of colors and fabrics covered the man's body from tip to toe. His feet peeked out and were covered with fur, leather, and twine. A worn felt hat covered his long white hair.

"Your boy is fine," he said. "He wandered on the path and came upon me at the pool of water. He asked if he could take a drink." There was a soothing, almost musical tenor to his voice. The old man had a hairless, wrinkled face and surprising blue eyes that reflected the water in the pool, calm and welcoming. His eyes reminded her of the Pachamama painting from the hotel. In the pool there were some plants springing from the bottom and floating with brilliant orange blooms at the top.

Astonished, she said to Mark, "Ryan talked to him?"

Mark shook his head. "I can't believe it. Never knew him to speak to strangers."

"Everyone down the mountain." Art interrupted. He attempted to corral them toward the path.

The man stood firm and addressed Mark and Sydney. "You can call me Pa'qo. I am shaman for the people. Man of medicine and spirit. I am the one you have been looking for."

His smile revealed warmth and a few missing teeth.

Mark was taking rapid, shallow breaths. "Thank you for finding my son."

Sydney glanced at Mark's wrist monitor. It was in the red zone. His patch needed to be replaced. "Let's get down to the lab so you can get another OID."

Pa'qo bent down to the edge of the water, tore off a cup-like leaf filled with water and handed to Mark. "Here, drink."

Mark sipped the liquid and his breathing steadied.

CHAPTER
TWENTY-THREE

h-ODD 535
Oxygen level 20.4

"I want to see Pa'qo today." Ryan announced the next morning to his father in between munching on fruit and granola. Mark had a hard time understanding Ryan's complete acceptance of this man. How did this happen? Did he miss some major change that caused Ryan to become more social? But even more important, he needed to understand why Ryan ran off yesterday. These mountain paths were not for the inexperienced and naïve. When he had raced up the path yesterday intent on finding Ryan, he didn't fail to notice the serious dangers in a place they knew nothing about. Part of him agreed with Art that none of them should be wandering off.

"Ryan, before we talk about Pa'qo I need to ask you about why you ran up the path to the mine yesterday?"

Ryan grabbed another aguaymanto from the bowl on the table and started to peel off the thin skin. His lips puckered when he placed the soft fleshy fruit in his mouth.

"Ryan, it's okay. You're not in any trouble. I'm not angry. Just worried about you. You know how much I love you. I got scared." He waited. He knew Ryan needed time to put his thoughts together.

Ryan swallowed. He wiped his fingers on the dark jeans he wore every day, looking down at where his hands now stayed resting on his lap. He let out a heavy sigh with shoulders shrugged and rocked back and forth in his chair. Mark leaned closer so he could hear what Ryan whispered, "I want to help."

This was going to take some time. "You want to help me?"

"Everyone." He tilted his head and looked up at his father. "I want to help everyone. No one lets me help. I can you know. Mom knew that."

Catherine had shared situations in her clinic with Ryan. Never naming names but giving him "puzzles" to solve. They both came to realize that this was who Ryan was. A genius puzzlesolver. Mark remembered the first time when she had a client who was having a hard time adjusting his medications and the man would often end up abandoning all of them and reverting to illegal drugs. Mark had heard her describing this to Ryan. Ryan absorbed it all. He found her old school textbooks from boxes in a basement closet and studied the physiology of drug interaction. He surprised both when at the dinner table one night he suggested a drug combination along with a nutrition-based diet. Catherine consulted with her colleagues. They agreed it was worth trying. It worked.

From that point, Ryan looked forward to and loved being a part of Catherine's work. She had respected his ideas. Respected him.

"Yes, your mom did know that you wanted to help." Mark moved his hand to Ryan's shoulder and squeezed. "I'm guessing you were feeling that we should be including you and you got upset?"

Ryan squirmed.

"I think it's about time you knew exactly what we're doing here." Mark scraped his chair on the wood floor. "Do you understand what's happening with the oxygen in the atmosphere?"

"I know about the diatoms being infected and how that hurts the atmosphere." Ryan's voice became serious as it did when he considered a new puzzle. "And I know the solution that you and Sydney want to do is with DNA. That's why we are up here. It's about Pa'qo and his people. The way their DNA works."

"Yes, that's right."

Ryan twisted in his chair and a moment later blurted out, "What I don't see is how CRISPR works to make someone's DNA go into another person. Describe that to me, Dad."

"Okay. I can explain that and you can ask me questions. How does that sound?" Ryan nodded. His face became a blank slate. Mark had seen this expression before. It was when he was readying himself for turning on his computer-processing mind.

"CRISPR is a method of genome editing. . ."

"Wait!"

"What is it? Isn't this what you wanted to know?"

"Yes, but does CRISPR stand for something? I want to know everything."

"Oh, okay. It's a bit technical, but CRISPR stands for Clustered Regularly Interspaced Short Palindromic Repeats." Mark took a breath and gazed over at Ryan.

He waited, shaking his head up and down, encouraging his father to continue.

"CRISPR is a method of genome editing," he began again, "that takes advantage of a natural DNA-snipping enzyme in bacteria, called Cas9, and that stands for CRISPR associated protein 9, to target and edit particular genes."

"Yes, yes. But how does it do it? How does it edit?"

Ryan never failed to impress him. His ability to process and understand was far beyond any other eleven-year-old. "The targeted sequence of DNA, the place where you want to change, is found by matching that sequence in a guide RNA molecule that is carried alongside the CRISPR associated protein 9." Ryan's eyes were wide-open; he was concentrating on every word. "Once found, the complex, the guide RNA and the Cas9, attaches to the matching DNA sequence and finds the spacer between the DNA genome sequence and 'cuts' the double strands. Here is when the programmed DNA is inserted into place."

"Pa'qo and his people have the DNA sequence that you want. The one you want to insert. They have the sequence that can breathe the air – even when the oxygen levels are low." It wasn't a question. Ryan had made the leap to the next logical progression.

Mark's pride showed in his face. His son was amazing. "That's right. We're collecting samples from some volunteers now. And we are creating the guide RNA and Cas9 complex and injecting it into cells."

Ryan jumped off his chair and gave him a quick hug. Then backed away. "I want to see Pa'qo today."

Mark laughed. Ryan was back to being a boy with his original request to see Pa'qo.

"Well, have you asked Pa'qo?" Ryan's autism didn't make teaching the subtleties of manners an easy task. Ryan had stopped acting out years ago thanks to Mark's soothing way of talking and Dr. Judson's behavior therapy. But Ryan needed gentle reminders at times.

"Yes, yes, I did. Yesterday at the pool he told me I could come."

"Was there a reason? Is he doing something special today?"

"Pa'qo is visiting his people today. He helps them."

Despite his reservations, it was clear Ryan was excited to see Pa'qo. And his son had spoken to the shaman, which alone was a breakthrough. He'd never seen him like this before.

Mark got up and refilled his coffee from the small pot. He had decided yesterday when he met Pa'qo to ask about acquiring more DNA samples from the people living there. He knew this was a task on Sydney's long list. She was wound tighter than a seaman's knot and he wanted to find a way to relieve some of her pressure.

"I'll take you by his house this morning and we'll talk to Pa'qo together."

TWENTY-FOUR

Mornings rolled into afternoons, and late nights in the lab became the routine. The work was tedious yet no one on the team complained. Thank heaven Mark had managed to speak with Pa'qo about the DNA samples. Sydney made a mental note to tell Pa'qo how much she appreciated his help. Pa'qo was becoming a key person in their CRISPR project. On top of all his shaman duties, he agreed to watch Ryan while Mark and the team worked long hours. She noticed how more relaxed Mark was during the day. It was evident that Ryan and Pa'qo had a bond and it pleasantly surprised her that Mark approved. She even felt a bit more at ease with the people here. When she'd observed the men and women marching toward the mines in the early morning fog, they seemed happy with their lives. Laughing at some joke, or embracing each other about shared good news. Never a bad word or, she surmised, any trouble among them. The people were closely connected and lived their lives in peace and harmony. Then there was Art. Art was the odd piece of this puzzle. He was a fish out of water here. He was difficult, to say the least. Particularly when she needed some extra supplies. He was the point person for anything coming in or going out of La Rinconada. A thought passed that perhaps he had taken the refrigeration units that went missing when Dar first got there. She shook that off. But there was no doubt his mantra seemed to be 'the world owes me'. She contemplated why someone would have such a giant chip on their shoulder. What could have happened in his life to make him so angry?

"Hey, Syd."

In the back of her mind, she heard a voice.

"SYD!" She looked up. Mark had leaned on her desk and was now waving his hand back and forth in front of her face.

"What? Something wrong with the edits? Something happen to someone?"

"No." Mark shook his head mumbling to himself, "Daydreaming again." He shifted his feet and took a step back, "No. Everything is coming along. No problems."

"Then what is it?" Sydney tensed her shoulders and her brows crinkled still anticipating something bad. She had a passing thought that he wanted to discuss Cuzco again.

"I need to finish some final test and I can't leave right now. It's after 5 and Ryan needs to be picked up from Pa'qo's."

She stared at him not quite comprehending what he wanted from her.

His face broke into a slight smile, I know this isn't your thing but I need you to get Ryan and bring him back here." He quickly added, "Dar is busy with the O$_2$ level reports and Yun left early today."

"Oh?"

"Only if you are available. I don't want to interrupt your work."

"No. I mean yes. I mean no, that's fine." She took a breath, "I can do that." She pushed back her chair with her head down, rushing out not wanting to see his giant grin.

Pa'qo had Ryan mixing some potions when she walked in. The place amazed her at its feeling of comfort and warm coziness. It was near freezing outside yet everything in here transported you to a place where you never wanted to leave. The smells, the dankness, the drudgery of the world all lifted away as you entered Pa'qo's home.

"Thank you again for watching Ryan. You are a god-send for our team."

"You and your team should be thanked for working on a most critical project for the earth." Pa'qo held out his hands to Sydney.

She wasn't sure what to do so she took both of his hands. He squeezed hers. She looked at their hands, "And thank you for organizing DNA samples from your people." She let go first and turned toward Ryan. "Are you ready to come back to the lab?"

On the walk back to the lab Ryan remained quiet. So different than a typical eleven-year-old boy who just spent a day mixing potions with a real-life shaman. She looked down at his soft curls picturing herself when she was his age. She had a strong urge to hug him close. Her childhood was filled with silence but also orders that constantly demanded her to 'one day become a famous scientist'. Ryan's world was silent too. But he had a good, kind mother. And of course, Mark, a wonderful father. At that moment a chilling breeze came across the tundra and instinctively she bent down to wrap her arms around Ryan and protect him from the harsh wind. He stiffened and she immediately dropped her arms afraid of how he would react. As she started to stand, she felt a small hand searching for hers. Her heart ached for, yearned for connection. And here was a young child who understood that. A tear pooled in the corner of her eye as they held hands walking back to the lab.

CHAPTER

TWENTY-FIVE

Back in California Sydney had asked Darweshi to do a more extensive check on Yun. But after they had arrived in La Rinconada, that work was overshadowed by everything else on their plates. Now after the incident with Ryan running up the path, instead of checking on Yun, she needed Darweshi to direct his digging efforts to the security officer. She was compelled to know what made Art so hostile toward her team. Some part of her brain kept ruminating about what was up with him. She didn't like surprises and knowing all the variables that could impact the project was part of her personality. That's how she controlled her world. Her curiosity also played a role. Perhaps a traumatic incident when he was young or past difficulty with the scientific community might explain the anger that emanated from him. When she mentioned this to Dar, he promised to do some high-level searches into Art's background. Sydney and Darweshi had built a close friendship from the start when she first hired him. He was a good man and loyal to her. She had suspected a long time ago that he might want more than friendship, but he never revealed anything other than that. She reflected on how much she depended on him over the years.

At the end of each day Darweshi would stop by her lab station or visit her room revealing any new tidbit that he unearthed. So far, he had found out Art had a normal childhood, at least according to the usual documentation. He was from Texas. A place called Kerrville. No juvenile records, no police cases. There was no missing parent, or abuse, or any records of medical conditions. Most of his life appeared normal. He even had a period where he was a Big Brother, soon taking on the role of head counselor at the Big Brother facility. At the age of thirty it appeared that he was set for life in that small town. Then suddenly he abandoned it all and joined the marines stationed in Indonesia and the South Seas. In another five years his life once again took a turn in a new direction. He was discharged from the marines and traveled to China. Sometime while in China he transferred to a special arm of the Western Hemisphere Coalition. This is where the documentation got vague. From bits and pieces of information Dar put together, Art had been completely out of communication with his superiors for six months during a global economic downturn in that part of the world.

"Maybe you should just give this up," Sydney said, shaking her head. "It's not like he's keeping us from doing what we came here for. I'm sure you overreacted during those first few days and I got caught up with finding out about him after Ryan had run away. I'm getting a bit uneasy with all this. You never know what we might find out."

"Isn't that the point?" He paused, "You know, Syd, I'll do whatever you want. But you may want to hear this before deciding to stop. Today I got in touch with a friend of mine who had some interesting information." It was late, about 9 p.m., and Darweshi was in Sydney's room. Sydney was sitting on the unmade bed and Darweshi was trying to get comfortable on the only wooden chair as he balanced the computer on his lap. "This computer is ancient." Darweshi placed his hands on the old-style keyboard. "Don't know why I even brought it but it's good for basic research. Okay got it." He said, "This time I have something solid. This old colleague of mine, Doug Obo, was in the same arm of the military as Art. I talked to him today and he sent me something that could shed light on the six-month mystery time when Art disappeared." Darweshi looked down at the computer and tapped a few keys to bring up an official looking document with a seal from the Western Hemisphere Coalition. "This guy, Doug, was in China the same time as Art working for the same agency, MCC. But he didn't know Art. They worked in different divisions."

"What is MCC?" She asked.

"Mandarin Central Consultants. Totally meaningless. You know these military acronyms."

Sydney got up from the bed and moved to look at the document filling the screen.

It was a government memo between two military officers.

"What's this?" She pointed to a handwritten note in the margin.

"Yeah. I saw that and can't make it out. It's too light."

"But maybe if we understand what's in the memo, we can make an educated guess about the note." Sydney was intrigued. She was a problem-solver. It was one of the reasons she was drawn to the Institute's work. Helping the earth using scientific solutions to the problems facing the world. It would've never worked out with Mark. Mark? Where did that come from?

She blinked and focused on the screen. "Look here," pointing to a place in the document where it mentioned the last location Art had been seen. "Where's this?"

"Harbin?" He tapped a few more keys. "That's in eastern China near the Russian border."

"Hmm. Look at the date."

"May 20, 2034." Darweshi shrugged.

"This date rings a bell." She pulled her thoughts together. Sydney had been in China with her mother during May of that year gathering financial support for the Institute. She remembered the devastation and the confusion in the region. "It was around the time the Chinese eastern railway was bombed. It was attributed to an ecoterrorist group. The railway was destroyed. Up to that date it was a major link for trade between China and Russia. That area plummeted into a recession for years. Art was there?"

"Seems that way."

Sydney now took another look at the faded handwritten note. She thought she could make out one word. "Does this word look like 'captured' to you?"

"Well, it might be. The 't' isn't crossed, and the last two letters are too faded. But it certainly looks like 'captured' now that you mention it."

Sydney got up from the bed thinking about what might have happened to Art. Her reasoning told her he was probably held prisoner somewhere in the Far East. But for how long? And how did he get out? She heard some horrible stories of prisons there. Physical torture and cruel mental pain. After an hour of more research and some handwriting-enhancing software the words became clear in the margin; *Asset captured. Do not negotiate. Delete from all records.*

"Whoa!" Darweshi blurted out.

"He was captured and held prisoner!" Why had the Western Coalition abandoned him?

Maybe here was the reason why Art was hostile. He had been abandoned by an organization that he had committed his loyalty and his trust to. But still, what was he doing in China in the first place? And how did he get out of prison?

TWENTY-SIX

That evening and at the same time Sydney and Darweshi were delving into Art's background, Mark finished up on some last notes regarding his work for the next day. Under a dim lamp he sat on his bed and closed his notebook. Ryan slept in the bed next to him, tucked under piles of blankets. He had been relieved when his discussion a few days ago with Pa'qo helped the team gather more DNA. When he first approached the shaman at his home, he thought Pa'qo was going to throw him out.

"We are not uneducated people. You cannot simply request something like DNA without giving an explanation. I did not like that you already convinced some of my people to give their DNA."

"It was an unforgiveable misstep on our part. I can see how wrong this was, arrogant of us to expect it would be handed over without any explanation." Mark paused waiting for Pa'qo to make the next move. If the shaman didn't agree to this, it could possibly delay or even shut them down.

"I am their leader spiritually, and similar to your government, politically."

"I'm so very sorry. Sydney, me, her team, we are all here for critical reasons. Reasons that have to do with the future of humankind, of all life on earth. We aren't here to hurt anyone. You must believe me, Pa'qo, if there was another way to do this we would. I can't reveal the science of what we're doing so I need you to trust me. Again, I'm so sorry we didn't come directly to you first."

The shaman had spoken to the villagers after Mark's visit and several agreed to provide samples. Sydney mentioned how she had thanked Pa'qo when she picked up Ryan for him. That was good. Pa'qo should hear it from her. The ones they had gathered were enough, but it was good to have more. Better to be extra careful and prepared. He got up, checked on Ryan and tiptoed to the hallway bathroom to wash up before going to bed. Sydney was never far from his thoughts. He resolved to have a serious discussion with her after they were back in California. Catherine was gone. He had loved his wife -- no one could replace her. But he had feelings for Sydney. Feelings, he admitted, that never truly went away.

The next morning a knock on the door cut into Mark's dream. In it he had been holding a glass vial and had set it down carefully before he walked toward Sydney. She kept moving away as he tried to get closer. The faster he went toward her the farther away she was.

He cleared the dream from his head and went to the door.

"Good morning!" Pa'qo stood there with that smile. "I have come to tell you how your son saved two lives yesterday." He stepped through the doorway. Mark was glad to see all the irritation from the DNA discussion gone from Pa'qo's demeanor. Pa'qo seemed as content as when he first met him a few days ago. Mark had been reluctant to have Ryan spend most of the day with Pa'qo but seeing first-hand the dramatic changes in his son he knew in his heart this was right. Still, he required that Pa'qo check in and report on Ryan every few hours.

"Good morning." Mark squeezed his eyes a few times. He could feel the sweat on his forehead from the dream. "What?"

Without missing a beat, Pa'qo continued, "I offer you much thanks for allowing Ryan to accompany me yesterday on my visits. It was Pachamama working through your son."

Mark shook his head. "What? What happened?" Pa'qo's words were finally sinking in. He realized he didn't get a report from Pa'qo yesterday. "Ryan didn't say a word when he came back." Mark sat back down on the bed. "And who is Posh-a-mamma?"

"PA-chuh-ma-muh" He slowly pronounced. Pa'qo folded his hands together in prayer. "She is our earth-mother, worshipped by our ancient culture, the Incas, and to this day is considered the reason for sustained life on earth. She watches over all the people."

Mark filed away this little piece of Andean culture to discuss later with Sydney. He was much more concerned right now with Ryan and how he'd saved two lives "Tell me what happened." Mark's body tensed.

"He is such an eager student, learning everything about the sacred medicines and herbal potions of the Andes. Do you know he has memorized many of the Andean potion names and what they are used for? In one day? He is very good with the people. I introduced him yesterday to several villagers saying he is my young assistant."

"Good with people?" That can't be Ryan. Now he was confused. He scratched his head.

"Sorry Pa'qo I don't understand. How did he save two lives?"

"After my work in the village I told him we were done for the day. I went to my kitchen to cook more medicines. He came back in minutes, stomping his feet and speaking in half words, 'wrong . . . dying . . . now'. He wanted me to follow him, even grabbed my sleeve to urge me." Pa'qo continued. "I asked Ryan, 'Who is it? Who is not well?' I managed to interpret Ryan's words that Azucena was having her baby and her husband Dario was crying. Ryan said, 'I must bring you to her now'."

"What was wrong?"

"It was not good for Azucena. She was not ready yet."

"Did you get there on time? What about the baby?" Mark tried to hurry Pa'qo along.

Clearly, the shaman liked to take his time when telling a story.

Pa'qo took Mark's hand in his and held it. "Ryan saved them both. I got to them and was able to give her medicine. Thanks to Pachamama and Ryan, an hour later Azucena and Dario had a healthy baby girl."

Mark sat and listened as Pa'qo praised Ryan and sent prayers of gratitude to the earth mother. It was hard to believe that within a few days his son had made leaps in his ability to deal with strangers and handle stressful situations. It's like he was finding himself here. "He has a great gift." Pa'qo nodded his head and smiled. "He is becoming one with the people."

After Pa'qo left, the story of Azucena quieted whatever remained of Mark's apprehension in leaving Ryan with Pa'qo. It was clear Ryan was making progress. Ryan needed to have influences from other role models. Even Dr. Judson had encouraged that Ryan's circle of people expand to others.

The next evening Mark was exhausted from another full day at the lab. They were now at the most delicate stage of attaching the blueprint into the cells. It took complete concentration. He tilted his head side to side to relieve the muscle spasms from looking down through a microscope all day. He went over to Ryan who was shuffling his feet on the floor of their room.

"So, after I left this morning what did you and Pa'qo do?" Mark was sensitive to questioning everything that went on with Ryan and Pa'qo. He wanted no more surprises. Ryan shrugged his shoulders and backed up to his bed. Mark was ready to collapse but something about Ryan's energy worried him. Mark hadn't seen him like this since California. His son was anxious about something.

"Ryan? What happened?"

"Pa'qo delivered a baby girl to Azucena and Dario. He works in the mine."

"Yes. . .Pa'qo told me. That was yesterday, right?"

"Pa'qo said it was difficult for Azucena but he gave her quechua and prayed to Pachamama. He explains to me about his spirit medicine."

Ryan slipped beneath the covers on his bed. This was one of his escape maneuvers.

Going to bed, dragging the covers over his head.

"It's okay, Ryan. You don't have to tell me, only if you want to."

Mark walked over to the bed and sat next to him. His son rolled to face the wall and started to speak, "I was with Pa'qo today and we were coming back from Dario's house making sure the baby and Azucena were okay." Ryan took in a deep breath and closed his eyes. "A big cat cried from one of the bushes along the path. Pa'qo wasn't afraid because he said the cry was one of pain, not anger."

Mark's hair on the back of his neck stood up. Ryan spoke louder and continued to take deep breaths after each sentence.

"Pa'qo said the puma was not okay. Pa'qo said the puma had poison in him. Someone gave him something bad."

"Did Pa'qo go near the big cat?"

"No, not then. He brought me back here first. You were at the lab, but Yun was in his room and said he would watch me. Pa'qo needed to go back and help. Give the puma a medicine so he wouldn't have so much pain. But he told me he would die. He said the large female with the black spot on her forehead would be sad. It was one of her cubs."

Mark took Ryan in his arms and rubbed his back to soothe the anxiety built up there. "I'm sure Pa'qo did whatever he could to help the animal. Now, how about I get you a glass of water and we talk about all the new potions and names you are learning from Pa'qo?" Mark wondered if the poison was natural, maybe a poisonous plant. It certainly couldn't have been a person who did this. And not deliberately. Why would someone deliberately poison a puma?

CHAPTER
TWENTY-SEVEN

h-ODD 1223
Oxygen level 20.3

Sydney bounced out of her bed and jumped in the shower. The team was making progress and now that Pa'qo had offered his assistance and collected DNA samples, her mind could concentrate on other parts of the plan. She found herself thinking that she was glad Mark was here. When he talked to her about Ryan's progress with Pa'qo, he also mentioned that Dario and Azucena had a baby girl. Apparently, Ryan was the reason the baby was here earlier than expected, and healthy. Most mornings since she arrived in La Rinconada she'd go for a quick run. Life here at the top of the Andes was so different than anything she ever knew. The runs kept her connected to the life she was used to in California. But today she'd forget the run and stop by and see Azucena; wish her well and congratulations. She didn't know her well but the short conversations at the boarding house encouraged her. She liked the woman and was curious to know more about her life here.

As she approached the small home, a short walk from the boarding house, she heard the soft cries of a newborn. The other children were outside on their way to the local schoolhouse. They waved to her as she walked up to the door.

Sydney waited at the door wondering if this was a good time to visit. She knew nothing of babies and didn't want to be a burden to the new mother. When she heard the cries stop, she knocked softly. Footsteps approached and an exhausted-looking Azucena opened the door. Her eyes told the story of a long night and her clothes looked like it'd been days since she changed. But Azucena smiled as she recognized who was at the door.

"Good morning, Azucena." Sydney whispered hoping not to disturb the sleeping infant.

"Buenos Dias, Señorita Davis. Do you need something? More towels? Or something else? Dario just left for the mines."

"No, no, Azucena. Everything is wonderful. I'm fine. I simply wanted to wish you all the best on your new baby girl."

"Ah! Gracias," Azucena pushed the door all the way open and stepped aside so Sydney could walk into the small space, "please come in."

Sydney remained at the doorstep. "Maybe this isn't the best time for a visit. I'm sorry. I can come back later."

"No, No. It's a good time. The baby will sleep for hours. She kept me up most of the night and now she's finally into a deep sleep." Azucena reached her hand out to Sydney and touched her arm, "Please come in."

The house looked warm and inviting. The wood stove provided an amazing amount of heat throughout the three small rooms. She led Sydney to a high back stuffed chair.

"Camila is our little angel, but she also is very demanding." Azucena stifled a yawn.

"Truly, I can come back later."

Azucena shook her head, "No. I'm very happy you are here. Can I get you coffee?"

"I'll get some at the lab. But thank-you. I wanted to congratulate you on your new little girl and to tell you how much I appreciate you and your family. You and Dario have been kind to me and my team."

"Of course." She smiled as she sat into the rocking chair.

Sydney's curiosity bubbled up as she sat and looked at the sparse room. She heard the wind slip through the wood of the only window in the room and thought about how a family survived in an environment like this. The words came out before she could stop, "How long have you lived here with your family?"

"Oh my, Dario was born here." Azucena's face brightened, "I was living in Puno when we met at the spring ceremony for Pachamama. We were both fourteen. I moved up here when he asked me to marry him."

"He is a very kind man. He helped Darweshi get settled when we needed to get the lab organized. It's a difficult environment for us to work in. Um . . . how do you manage so well with the weather and the altitude?" Sydney hoped she didn't offend.

Azucena looked out the one window in the tiny room. She turned to Sydney. "Do you know Pachamama?"

Sydney furrowed her brows, confused. What did their deity have to do with surviving in La Rinconada? "Yes, I first saw a painting of her in a hotel in Cuzco. I did a little research. She is your earth goddess. But how does she help you to exist here?"

Azucena shook her head and smiled as if she was dealing with one of her children. "Pachamama becomes our eyes that allow us to see, she is our mouth so that we speak the truth, she is our hands and our feet so that we can work and give thanks. She is at the heart of everything we do. It doesn't matter where we are, she is always with us."

"But why are you here?"

"Because this is where we are needed. Where we are guided by *Buen Vivir*, the Good Life. We are here in this environment to offer respect, community, solidarity, and harmony. It is here that we promote our culture, educate our children, and offer our spirit to Mother Earth. We are not political nor involved in the workings of the world but we are connected to the environment here. We are both human and earth here. Someday the gold mining will be gone and we will still be here respecting the land and every living thing that exists. No, there is no other place for us."

For a moment Sydney saw the beauty of what she described. Transcendence through nature rather than religion. These people were connected by nature, their shared culture, and their combined belief in Pachamama.

Camila's cries broke Sydney's thought and Azucena jumped out of her chair to attend to her newborn.

After Sydney left, she more closely considered Azucena's words. They lived as one with the earth. The lines between hard science and spirituality were blurred here. Science was spiritual and spirituality was science. They didn't just exist on the earth; they were of the earth.

TWENTY-EIGHT

Dr. Davis's com-call that morning was scratchy, "So then, everything's moving forward and on schedule. Good! When are you testing and validating the result?" Davis didn't give Sydney a chance to confirm or deny. Her mother received daily, sometimes twice a day status updates. Sydney had expected pressure from her mother. She knew Davis reported back after these calls to people around the globe. Sydney took a deep breath. The critical path of the CRISPR edit was on everyone's mind. The process to mass produce and distribute to the human population required at least three months. Their schedule required two days to develop the prototype gene injections. Four days were already gone. The projected atmospheric reports from Darweshi earlier were not good. They showed an increasing downward trend of oxygen levels. The latest reports were down 0.02. Maybe she should double-check his numbers.

"Ready to test." Sydney kept it short, "There has, however, been a delay with the test subjects who will be getting the gene edit." The van broke down carrying the volunteer subjects traveling up from Puno. They were the critical and final piece of the project. These volunteers would get the CRISPR injection of the altered gene from the blueprint of the locals and then be tested whilst breathing low oxygen levels. If they had no adverse reactions, the team could pack up and go back to California to begin the mass production and distribution process. The volunteers were supposed to arrive this morning. "The van broke down . . ."

Davis didn't wait for any further clarification, "Just get it done…today." Silence. Davis disconnected the call. As always, she expected no pushback, especially from Sydney.

Sydney sat back in her chair and mentally played back the early morning call from the van driver.

"Are you telling me no one can go up or down the mountain right now?" Sydney had swung around spilling the contents of her morning coffee over her work area just missing the computer. She listened to the scratchy voice of the man who had brought them to La Rinconada explain the freak breakdown. The service had made it barely audible.

"You're saying a rockslide had you swerve and something scraped the bottom of your van?"

"Si. Señorita Davis. The van ran over the rocks and broke an axle."

"Where are you now?"

"We were only five miles up the mountain. We are now hiking down the mountain path back to Puno."

Sydney drummed her fingers and debated what to do next. She had to do the test with the volunteers today. She reluctantly decided to try Art; see if he knew about this; could maybe even help. She picked up her phone and dialed his security shack number.

No answer. She wondered if he already knew. Afterall he wasn't happy about strangers coming into his domain.

CHAPTER
TWENTY-NINE

The incident with the volunteers and the van intensified Sydney's investigation of Art. She hesitated to accuse him of any wrongdoing without concrete evidence. Dar continued his pursuit into Art's past with Sydney's blessing.

After he had found out about Art's past with MCC, Darweshi focused on his life after the incident in China. Sydney expected him to find things like records of a disgruntled employee or perhaps an incident revolving around a personal grudge against the government. However, Darweshi began reporting back on serious pieces of information – like an article of Art being involved in a weapons black market raid when he was in Singapore and then soon after another article about him living in South Africa and being brought up on charges for stealing high-end military electronics; stuff used in explosions. There was something going on here in La Rinconada – just as Darweshi first suspected when he arrived and witnessed the incident in the warehouse.

The following day, after reporting to Sydney the latest on Art, Darweshi carried on digging for more information. Later that afternoon he rushed into the lab and went directly over to Sydney and whispered, "I poked around and found that sulfuric acid, the runoff byproduct of gold mining machinery, is unregulated by the government here. There is no contained process in this location for capturing the run-off. It just goes down through the mine and either is absorbed or runs into one of the small streams." Darweshi clenched his fist. "How can they let this happen?" He shook his head back and forth and continued, "Anyway, that made me wonder if Art was collecting and selling the liquid. Why else would he have those barrels in his private warehouse? I did more sleuthing and discovered sulfuric acid can be used to synthesize explosives. I decided last night to talk to Dario. What I saw that first night in the warehouse with Dario made me think that he might help us. He must know the connection."

"What? Sulfuric acid? Explosives? Like TNT?"

"Yeah. Explosives. I knew there must be some connection to Art. I waited for Dario to leave the mines last night."

"You don't think Dario is involved with Art in this, do you?"

"No, not a bit. He's a good guy. I'm sure."

"You talked with him last night? What happened?"

Darweshi shrugged his shoulders. He lowered his voice, "I decided to ask him a few questions."

Darweshi had waited behind some brush and stopped Dario on the mine path when he felt that everyone was out of earshot. Everyone rushed down the path eager to get home to their families and enjoy some warmth before coming back to the drudgery the next day. No one had given him a second look.

"Hey Dario!" Darweshi was a few feet away. Dario stopped short and peeked up with hooded eyes under his mining helmet.

"I'll come right to the point." Darweshi scratched his forehead and took a long breath. "When I first came here, I did some snooping around one night. I found a warehouse way in the back of town. I saw you there."

Dario stiffened and spun his head around looking up the path to the warehouse.

Darweshi held up his hands. "Hey Dario, we're friends, you, and me. I would never do anything to hurt you or your family. You're good people. Dario, please listen." Darweshi waited for Dario to respond.

Dario paced back and forth on the path. Looking up toward the mine and back at Darweshi. After a long minute of pacing, "Bueno. What is it you want to know?" Dario faced Darweshi and dropped his voice to a whisper.

"We're doing some really, really, important work here. And I need to know what Art's involved in so we can be sure it won't impact what we're doing." Darweshi noticed that Dario stiffened his shoulders. "Please Dario, can you tell me anything about what Art's doing with the sulfuric acid he's collecting?"

"I never wanted to be part of this, Señor Darweshi. Señor Saunders told me I must, or I lose my job and, well, five niños and one new baby, I had no choice. Si?"

"I understand and I won't say anything about you and your family to anyone. What's Art doing? Is it illegal?"

Dario's shoulders relaxed after taking one last look around. The shift was well into the next. No one was left on the path. "Si, illegal."

"Does Art sell the sulfuric acid to people for money?"

"Si."

"Does Katen know about this?"

"No, no." Dario shook his head vigorously.

"Do you have any idea what these people Art sells the acid to are using it for?"

Dario looked up at the sky. He seemed as though he was trying to find a word. Dario finally said in a low voice. "Explosions."

"Damn." Darweshi had rubbed his hand across his bald head. "I knew it." Darweshi needed more but was concerned Dario had had about enough of his questions. He put his hand out to shake. "Thank you."

Sydney wrinkled her forehead when Darweshi finished telling her what he'd found out. Disturbingly, during one of their background searches they had discovered the mention of TNT being used in the railway explosions where the terrorists died in China. There were reports indicating traces in the debris.

CHAPTER
THIRTY

"I'm not sure what I can do from here. I received direct information from the US government that this is important work. I've approved whatever project you have going on there." Wallace Katen emphasized the word 'whatever'. Sydney had called him and explained the issue with the van and the delay hoping he could help. He continued, "But they won't disclose anything else. What else can I do?"

"I apologize that this is requiring so much time and secrecy, but we'll be done in a few days. This is the last step. I only need to conduct the tests on the subjects that had gotten stuck on the mountain. I need them here as soon as possible. I promise after that, we'll be gone."

"Can't you work through Art? He is my man there."

"It would be a great help if Art could go and pick them up. Or maybe you can send some other men? They only need some parts for the van." Sydney didn't want to reveal Art's side business. When Darweshi had revealed what he found out, he had said there was more, but Sydney had been preoccupied with the test subjects.

Speaking with Katen now she wanted him to offer some help, maybe some other security people. She hoped he wouldn't question her further.

"You're still not answering my question. Why didn't you tell Art and get him to do this?" Katen insisted.

Sydney felt trapped. She was stuck in place while the clock ticked away. A decision had to be made. She had an inkling that Art knew they knew something. Darweshi isn't the most subtle person. Art's operation of collecting sulfuric acid and selling it on the black market made huge sums of money. Darweshi told her that sulfuric acid was more tightly controlled since 2030 yet there were no regulations on governing excesses and waste. Darweshi had done some estimates and Art's side business made over five figures a week. She had every intention of reporting him once they were done with the gene injections. Unfortunately, there was no getting around this, ethically she had to tell Katen about Art.

Her voiced lowered. "I... well, we found some disturbing news about Art and the mine."

"What news?" Katen's voice exploded and she could picture him jumping up from his comfortable chair in his office suite.

"Please Mr. Katen, we had no intention of getting involved in your business but the circumstances. . ."

"Just tell me. Is my business in danger? Has something happened to the mine? To Art?"

"It's about Art." She hesitated. Not sure how much she should reveal.

"Dr. Davis! What is it?"

"We discovered he is running a black market for sulfuric acid which I'm sure you're aware is a by-product of gold mining. He's been selling the liquid and using some of your local miners under duress to help with his operation." It came out like rushing water. She couldn't stop once started.

She heard breathing. Then his voice burst through the phone.

"I don't believe it. I can't believe it."

"I'm sorry but we've confirmed it with one of the locals." He'd probably be more apt to believe the locals than her.

"I'm sending Katen officials down there tomorrow. I knew I shouldn't have hired him. He was never my first choice, but no one else was even remotely interested in doing the job there. Damn!" She heard his fist bang against something and glass shattered. "My men will be there tomorrow and take care of him. You just stay away from this until they get there." He disconnected the phone.

It appeared that her test subjects would not be in La Rinconada any time soon. The project couldn't wait until tomorrow. She needed to do something today. Sydney looked at her calendar. Today was Christmas Eve. She decided to give the team a few hours to call family or friends. She needed that time to work through this delay on her own. She went to the lab and notified everyone about the time off. Yun jumped off his lab stool and raced toward the boarding house. Mark laughed and grabbed her in a hug, "Ryan really needs this, thanks."

Taken by surprise, she put her hands up and backed away. Mark stared at her. For a moment, a hurt expression crossed his face. After a few seconds he said "I can't leave you with this work. We are almost there."

"Please go. Spend a few hours with Ryan. I'll recheck the injections. Just one person is needed. Go."

Mark left and the lab was empty. She plopped onto her desk chair and leaned back.

"Syd, I need to tell you something."

She tipped dangerously close to falling over backward but caught herself before completely losing balance. "Dar? Don't sneak up like that. Can it wait? So much to do before tomorrow."

Dar ignored her remarks and pressed on, "I tried to tell you before. There is something else I found out when I was looking into Art's past. I discovered the names of the people killed in that explosion with the railway. I recognized one in particular."

"And?" Sydney barely heard him. She turned away and began typing into the computer.

"Li Chin, Yun's older brother."

Her fingers froze. "Who? Yun? Our Yun? Are you sure?" This couldn't get any worse.

Was it a coincidence or was there a connection?

"Yeah. Positive. His brother was part of an eco-terrorist group back then. He helped to plan the bombing and I guess found himself at the short end of the stick."

"What's going on here?" She tightened her fist on the desk. Her face flushed, her mind full of questions, "Do you know anything else? Is Yun involved with this group?"

"Don't know. But I'll keep looking." He left.

This was too much. There is a tipping point, and she was about there. She pushed away the thoughts of Yun and his brother for now and concentrated on completing the test trial. With no other choice, she made the decision to enact her contingency plan. Something she didn't want but now needed to do.

CHAPTER
THIRTY-ONE

h-ODD 2367
Oxygen level 20.4

It was midnight. She waited until she was sure everyone would be sleeping. She stood at the refrigeration unit in the dimly lit lab. The CRISPR injection needles were lined up and ready to go--ready to test on subjects. Subjects that were delayed. Her team worked hard to get to this point and this was the only path forward. She grabbed one of the injections and walked to the lunchroom. She needed some caffeine to keep her awake. She had to make sure she stayed alert when she injected the DNA into her bloodstream. Pouring a cup, she sank into the armchair facing the window with a view of La Bella Durmiente. As she slipped off her OID and sipped coffee, she looked out at the glacier named 500 years ago by the locals. Sleeping Beauty. Ironic, since this location looked more like a beast -- desolate, grey, imposing. Its massive size overlooked La Rinconada and gave her a feeling of an other-worldly presence.

"Hey. Burning the midnight oil?" It was Mark.

She jolted upright. Was she relieved to hear his deep baritone? "Couldn't sleep. Thought I'd check on the temperature in the units. Just made coffee. Want some?" She said as she pushed the injection needle between the cushions of the chair hiding the movement before Mark walked into view.

"Sure," he said. Sydney made a motion to get up while burying the needle further into the cushion. "No, you stay there. You look too comfortable. I'll get it." He looked at her sideways. "You never offer to get me a coffee. Must be feeling magnanimous these days." He laughed and walked to the pot and emptied the rest of the pots' contents into his cup. He lifted it to his lips and sniffed. "We need better coffee." He shrugged and gulped it down.

"So, you couldn't sleep either? Where's Ryan?"

"He wanted to stay overnight with Yun and Darweshi. He and Yun have a contest going on with that game. Darweshi seemed to be fine with it. Plus, I think it helps to encourage Ryan to be comfortable with others. Believe it or not, coming to La Rinconada has been a turning point for him."

"Yes, I heard about how he has been working so well with the shaman." Sydney truly was happy for Mark. Looking at his face, she could tell this was a breakthrough. He was beaming. Even she felt some of that pride. Ryan was exceptional. He had a heart and was brilliant. She had witnessed both thinking back to the day he took her hand. A very special connection between them started that day.

"Pa'qo has been taking him along on his medicine rounds through the village." Mark sat on the arm of the chair nearest her. Sydney moved her body so the needle was totally hidden. "Oh, I wanted to ask you about this deity called . . .wait like me get this right . . . Pachamama.

Pa'qo mentioned this earth goddess. Have you read anything or heard about her?"

Sydney, glad to distract him, quickly took up the subject. "I read about Pachamama after seeing the painting at the hotel in Cuzco. I wondered at the power of spiritual connections and the locals' belief in her. I talked with Azucena a little about it. I've been meaning to do more research but right now isn't the best time." She made a motion with her hand toward the lab alluding to everything that still needed to be done. The moon shone through the window illuminating her hand and she felt the gritty cold creep in through the cracks. She remembered looking at the moon that night in California when the idea first came to her about changing human DNA. Was it a week ago? They had worked non-stop from the moment they arrived. Mark struggled to stand. He grunted and fell to the floor tipping over the chair. At the same time, Sydney felt herself drifting off. She had a strange taste in her mouth. Like bitter greens from the garden, it was probably the coffee. She shook her head a few times. "Mark. Mark? What's wrong? Mark!" Her legs were heavy. Confused, she tried to pitch herself forward out of the chair to get to him. When her legs felt like they were in freshly poured concrete, she started to panic. "Move, dammit!" she yelled at her legs. "Mark!" He was silent and not moving.

Dizziness took over as her chin fell to her chest.

"You're not going anywhere."

A voice she recognized but couldn't place. Her brain was in a fog. Forcing past the dizziness, she lifted her head. A face appeared in front of hers, snake tattoo on the neck. "Art?"

"Did you think I'd just go away after you spilled my operation to Katen? That ass."

"I can't move my legs."

"Oh, I'm pretty sure you can't move anything right now."

Sydney attempted again to push herself up. Her arms went limp against her sides. Her mind wasn't registering what happened. She needed to call someone, anyone.

"I don't shrink into nowhere when someone goes against me. You cost me everything when you reported me to Katen. I've been working in this god-forsaken hole for five years!" Art swiped his arm across the lab table sending the delicate equipment crashing to the floor.

"Wha . . . what did yo . . . you . . . do to me? Mark?"

"When they find you tomorrow, I'll be long gone. My luck just got better when I saw him come in. Two for one." His hands flexed into fists, "Although I would've loved to beat him about first, but no time for fun." Art came forward and with his hand he grabbed her chin. He put his face inches from hers. "I put a little something in the coffee. Poison that I stole from the shaman. I keep it on hand in case one of the miners gets a conscience. Easy way to get rid of any threats."

"Poison?" Sydney's headed pounded.

"Yeah. I use it on the pumas occasionally to make sure it's still potent." His words spit out into her face, "But for you and your friend well, let's just say your burned bodies will be discovered because of an unfortunate accident. A fire will destroy everything in this lab. Nothing will be left."

Sydney struggled to focus. "No! No, you can't!"

"I can do anything I want. This is my town, my place. Or it was. But now, because of you I gotta leave; find another, somewhere far from here."

His eyes burned into hers. She couldn't believe what she had heard. She had no doubt now, he was insane. "F-f-fool!" she managed through her teeth, "the earth . . . p-people . . . will . . . die."

"Right, and you two will be the first. Followed by that kid, Yun." He stomped over to a can of something and began splashing it around the lab.

Sydney desperately looked over at Mark still slumped on the floor. A distant rumble started above her head and she saw Art turn toward the window following the noise. It quickly increased to a roar and everything went into slow motion. The mountain trembled. Ice mixed with rock and gravel crashed through the roof. The earth under her feet shuddered. She moved her eyes to find Art.

She choked. She was losing consciousness. Above the noise, she heard a voice calling out, "Sydney, Sydney!"

In the back of her mind, she felt arms lifting her. Her head fell back, then blackness.

CHAPTER
THIRTY-TWO

"Sydney, Syd can you hear me?" Someone stroked her hair and pressed fingers on the side of her neck.

Sydney could hear the voice faintly, but it became static in her head. Pieces of memory were there but a lot was missing. She remembered Mark came into the lab. They both drank coffee and there was a tremendous roar out the window. But what happened in between? Someone else had been in the lab with her. Her mind fog started to clear. Art! She pushed away the hand on her neck and struggled.

"Get away from me!" she screamed.

"Syd, it's me, Dar." He removed his fingers from her neck and moved so Pa'qo could examine her. "It's okay, you're gonna be okay, relax. We're all here, Mark too."

Sydney tried to lift on her elbows and looked around. Yun, Darweshi, Ryan, and Pa'qo stood around her.

Through the haze she saw bright orange and blue greens illuminating the room. She had a flash of recognition—it was the shaman's room. She'd had a quick visit when she picked up Ryan that day. Mark was sitting up in a large chair covered with an animal skin.

He had a bloody cut on his forehead.

"What happened? Where's Art? Did you see him?" She recalled bits and pieces still unsure if she was imagining Art in the lab. "The lab!" Her memory returned full force. She physically shrunk back from the memory of Art's hot breath on her face. "He was there, right next to me when the building shook like nothing I'd ever experienced before and then the floor beneath us collapsed." She searched Dar's face, "Art was there, angry at me! And Mark!"

"There was a landslide just as I predicted." Yun called out from the doorway.

"And no trace of Art."

Dar pulled a blanket over her and spoke to both her and Mark, "Art stole a plant concoction from Pa'qo." The small window in the room reflected the lamp light highlighting small twigs and bones hanging from the headboard. They rattled when she moved on the bed. On the table next to the bed, bottles of murky potions lined up. Pa'qo's house was filled with pieces of wood, stones, and bones, like art in a natural history museum.

Pa'qo stepped into her view with his head down, "I never lock the cabinet door where my medicines are kept. He came here and took the delicate plant, brugmansia from my potions. It affects the nervous system. I use it in small doses to keep my patient still like an anesthesia, when it is necessary." Pa'qo said shaking his head.

"Art used the poison on us." She shifted as the bones clattered louder to reach a hand to Mark. "Mark!" Something inside her head clicked. She paused. "Fire! He was going to set the lab on fire. Oh my god!"

Mark shifted to reach out. "There was no fire. And I'm fine, Syd. Ryan told me about a poisoned puma. It was a cub. Art used the animals as tests." Mark croaked from under the animal skin.

"Why were you both at the lab?" Darweshi interrupted.

"Ryan had told me he saw Art sneaking next to the lab when we were heading back to our rooms after Sydney gave us the night off. I decided to drop Ryan off at Pa'qo's and come back to check it out." Mark explained. "I found Sydney drinking coffee. Figured everything was in order."

"Evil man." Ryan whispered to Mark. Ryan sat close to his father. He was shaking.

Pa'qo looked down at Ryan and put his hand on his shoulder. Ryan's shoulders relaxed under this gentle pressure. He snuggled closer to his father. Sydney felt an ache for that kind of human connection. She slid herself up and leaned against the bed's backboard.

Pa'qo wrapped an arm around Ryan's shoulders gently prying him away. He looked back at Mark, "You both need to rest. I'll take care of Ryan."

Yun edged his way toward the door of Pa'qo's bedroom. Sydney caught the motion and suddenly recalled what Art had said just before the landslide. She jerked up and extended her arm and pointed, "Yun! Art said something about you!"

Mark got up and moved to Sydney. He attempted to ease her back down. "We'll figure out what Art's up to when we get him here. I'll worry about that. You need to rest."

Sydney pushed away from Mark, wide-eyed, "Oh, no! The injections!"

Darweshi ignored her and turned his head to stare out the small window. Yun was at the door and shuffled his feet on the wood floor. Sydney grabbed Mark by his pant leg, twisting the fabric in her fingers. "What happened to the CRISPR injections?"

No one spoke.

"Are there any left?" Her eyes searched Dar's face waiting for another answer to what she already knew.

"Gone. All of them," Darweshi said.

"So sorry. I would have tried to salvage some, but Pa'qo said it was too dangerous. The side of the building where the injections were stored was demolished," Yun said as he moved back into the room.

"I need to regroup. Figure out next steps." Her arms tingled as feelings returned to her extremities. She felt better. She looked over at Pa'qo. "Did you give me something?"

"It is a natural plant that I use for many purposes." Pa'qo kept his voice even.

"And it will counteract the effects of what I was given?"

"It will take time. But I will watch you and give you more as needed."

Mark stood on the side of the bed looking down at her. She could feel his stare. His question blurted out into the room, "What were you really doing there so late?" She couldn't answer this now. She needed to be alone. She needed time to process what happened and how she could get the project back on track. And she especially didn't want any questions about what she was doing at the lab and her contingency plan.

"So…" Mark started.

"I'm exhausted," She cut him off, "I need some rest."

"You need sleep," Pa'qo said to Sydney, "best for you. And for you."He nodded toward Mark.

"Thank you." She rested her head in the middle of the pillow.

Darweshi and Yun walked out of the small room. Mark went back to the chair and pulled up the animal cover. He gave her one more look. As soon as he did, Sydney closed her eyes. After a few minutes she peeked through one squinted eye. He seemed to be sleeping. She needed time to think.

CHAPTER
THIRTY-THREE

h-ODD 4021
Oxygen level 20.3

After Yun and Darweshi walked out Mark closed his eyes and pretended to sleep. He had wanted to question Yun about why Art would target him but there was too much happening right now. The most important question was why Sydney was in the lab. He had an inkling of what she planned to do but not why. He stepped over to her bed making no effort to be quiet.

Sydney's head snapped up as soon as he approached.

He let out a sigh. "What were you doing in the lab?"

Sydney opened her mouth to answer. He held his hand up to stop her. "Don't. What I need to understand is why?"

"I had to. I had no choice. The test results were expected. No, not expected, critical to keep us on track. Also, I found out before we left California that people were already starting to die of asphyxiation. People who are vulnerable. The numbers are accelerating. I had to do it."

"Don't you realize you're the crucial link on this team? You're crazy, risking everything by attempting this. I could've been the test subject!" He opened and closed his fists to release his anger. He was overcome with a need to protect her. He was about to continue his lecture when he stopped himself, "Why didn't you tell me about people dying?" The vein in his temple pulsated. "Syd?"

"I couldn't add more stress to everyone. We had to keep going without any distractions."

"And then you go and inject yourself!" Mark's voice lowered in exasperation.

Sydney turned her head away on the pillow, "I never did inject myself, but it makes no difference now. Everything has been destroyed. Mother can only blame me. I'm the one who caused this mess."

Mark's interactions with Dr. Davis were minimal. Over the two years at the Institute, he never said more than two sentences to her. This project gave him an opportunity to form an opinion of Sydney's mother and it was not a good one.

Sydney closed her eyes whispering to no one in particular, "What do we do now? This was our only hope."

"Well, there's another wrinkle in this mess."

"What wrinkle? What else happened?" She spun back toward him and raised herself up on her elbows.

"Ryan. He was distraught. When he told me about Art heading back to the lab, he mumbled something about Art being bad, and then he got frantic repeating, 'it will not work, the edit will not work.' I was anxious to find out what Art was up to, so I tried to calm him and brought him over to Pa'qo. Unfortunately, I didn't pay much attention to why he was agitated."

"Why would he say it wouldn't work?" She rubbed her hand over the blanket on the bed. It soothed her to feel the softness; she wanted to fall into it.

"I don't know. I'm still trying to sort that out. There are too many moving pieces."

Sydney threw her feet off the bed and attempted to stand. Her balance faltered and he tried to stop her. Her eyes rolled back in her head as she fell against him. The whole bed shook against the wall when they both fell onto the mattress. She didn't have on her OID and Mark quickly took off his patch and monitor and clasped it on her arm. Pa'qo drifted into the room without a sound, his arms full of local plants.

"Syd!" Mark said. He shook her shoulders. Her breathing was regular, but she was not responding. From the corner of the room Mark heard a low monotone chant as Pa'qo reached for plants with orange and black flowers from a cabinet. Mark had seen them along the mining paths. Pa'qo crushed them as he placed the leaves in a tray with a liquid that was slowly disintegrating them. It filled the room with a sweet pungent odor. Like gardenias in vinegar. Ryan appeared and ran toward his father. Ryan's arms were moving in fast jerky arcs. Mark soothed Ryan's movements by stroking his back and arms. Clenching his jaw, Mark turned to Pa'qo.

Pa'qo nodded reading his mind, "I will watch her."

Mark placed his arm around Ryan and led him out of the room with the melodic sound of Pa'qo's chanting.

When they were in the main room of the house, Mark knelt on the hard floor with his hands on Ryan's shoulders. His voice was soft. "Ryan, what is it you want to say?" He loved him so much. He wanted to take away all his pain, protect him.

Ryan wrung his hands as his voice got louder, "I knew it, I knew it, I knew it." Ryan would either yell words out loud or just whisper when he became anxious.

"Ryan, please, what did you know?" Mark released his son's shoulders.

"It's not going to work. I saw it. All pieces did not fit." Ryan jerked his body when Mark released him. Mark quickly put his hands back on Ryan's upper arms to steady him.

"Okay, it's okay."

"Pa'qo knows the ways. He fixes the people so they can live here. I should have told you sooner. If I told you sooner Sydney would be okay."

"Ryan you are not responsible for what's happened to Sydney. You've grown attached to her. I see that. I also see that you understand so much about Pa'qo and his medicine. I need to ask you a question."

Ryan shuffled his feet and nodded once.

"Does any of this have to do with the medicine Pa'qo gives his people?"

Ryan nodded.

"Mark! Please come here." Pa'qo's voice was loud and insistent.

Mark needed to speak with Ryan in a quiet environment. This wasn't going to happen until after he had Sydney safe and had Art locked away. He quickly walked back into Pa'qo's bedroom. Sydney looked like she was sleeping.

Pa'qo was mixing potions. "She fell into the otherworld place."

Mark rushed over and sat on the bed, touching her forehead. "I'll call the Institute and have them send a helicopter and get her to a hospital."

"You do what you have to, I will do the quechua." Pa'qo said. "Her reaction to the poison was worse than I hoped." He took one of the plants and held it up to the lamp. "Quechua is an ancient plant that grows only here. It has been used to cure many ailments of our people. I pray to the goddess, Pachamama." Pa'qo turned back to his patient.

Sydney needed medical attention right now regardless of Pa'qo's ancient medicine. Dr. Davis had to be called. Not to mention finding Art and stopping whatever other madness he intended. He needed to get Darweshi and Yun to help search for Art. Ryan huddled in a corner of the room with his eyes downcast.

Mark approached him with his hand extended. "Ryan, please stay here with Pa'qo. I need to make a com-call."

Mark spoke quietly. "We will talk soon, but right now, I need you to be strong. Can you do that?"

"For Sydney?" Ryan said.

"Yes, for Sydney. She'll be okay. I promise. Pa'qo will take care of her." Mark hugged him. "I love you very, very much." He looked over at Ryan as he stepped outside alone. He left Ryan and Sydney in the care of Pa'qo. The two people on this earth that he loved more than anything. The punch of the cold air hit his face and, for a moment, broke his concentration. He pulled himself together and initiated the call to Dr. Davis. Was it still December 25th?

CHAPTER
THIRTY-FOUR

"I love you very, very much." It was Mark's voice but Sydney couldn't place where they were. Her head pounded and her thoughts were jumbled. She felt the soft bed and the way it conformed to her body. She imagined the warmth of Mark's body snuggled against her back. Suddenly she was back in Boston. They had gotten back from celebrating their one-year anniversary of their meeting on the motor spinner. He had mentioned marriage earlier during dinner across the way-too-formal starched tablecloth that somehow contrasted with the softness of the candlelight reflecting in his eyes. He had a way of making all the weight of the world - her finals, her mother, her anger disappear. After dinner they went home, made love and he had fallen asleep. As she had listened to his relaxed breathing, she'd wondered why she didn't answer him. She knew she loved him too. She had been hesitant to say anything, holding back for reasons that she herself wasn't ready to know yet.

When he voiced his love for her and she didn't respond, he had simply squeezed her hand and nodded, "I can wait for you. I'll be here whenever you're ready."

Her visit to the gynecologist the day of the candlelight dinner was supposed to be a routine exam. For the next three days after Sydney dragged herself around their small apartment. She went through the motions of being normal waiting for the test results. But she was far from normal.

On the day of her physical, Dr. Condon asked her to wait when he had finished with the routine examination. He wasn't gone for more than a few minutes. She remembered thinking maybe that's good news.

"We're going to run a few extra tests this time. There are some growths." He must have seen her eyes pop out of her head. "Nothing to worry about yet."

The call came on the fourth day. She was alone in the apartment. Dr. Condon's voice was soft but scientific. He outlined several facts about why it would be unadvisable for her to have children.

Her initial reaction was to call Mark. He wouldn't be home for a few hours and she wanted to tell him in person so she waited. As the hours stretched by, she kept thinking about how he talked about a family at their celebration dinner. She knew he wanted children. He came from a big family – five brothers. And he loved every one of them. They were all so close; talked on the phone, sent gifts for holidays and birthdays. By the time he arrived home she had convinced herself that maybe telling him now wasn't a good idea. He would be crushed and his career was just taking off. He needed no distractions. The next week Sydney received the call from her mother regarding the position at the Institute.

THIRTY-FIVE

On the second day that Yun had arrived in La Rinconada, he discovered someone had gone through his stuff. Nothing was missing, but his game, *Surrection*, had been accessed. Yun had an activity detection app that had notified him of the breach with a date and time stamp. He had asked Darweshi about it, but Darweshi just shook his head and said, "I think we were both in the lab at that time." He shrugged his shoulders, "It was probably just some kids from the town." Yun wasn't so sure. He couldn't figure out how a kid had gotten through his password. He was not a person who was easily unsettled, but this was unnerving. *Surrection* was not just a game.

He headed back to the boarding house when he left Pa'qo's after the incident with Sydney at the lab. Bothered by the ominous news she had revealed about Art planning to come for him, Yun's head throbbed. He wondered if it was Art who had rifled through his room. Yet he couldn't fathom why Art would target him. Yun's reasons for being here were more than just the CRISPR project but no one else knew this except the few leaders of the eco-revolutionary group. He needed to contact them and let them know of a possible change in plans. Yun picked up his pace as he headed toward the boarding house.

When Yun got to the room he immediately went to his computer. With a few clicks and an encrypted password, his app, *Surrection*, filled the screen. He typed keeping an eye on the door. The last thing he needed was for Darweshi to walk in.

He sent a message that he may be compromised and asked if he should continue.

The plan had been engineered by the head of the group, Malcolm. No last name. When Yun had told Malcolm that he was heading to La Rinconada, Malcolm persuaded him that this was fate. Malcolm was charismatic and described La Rinconada as the worst offender of environmental concerns by many conservation groups. He preached that gold mining was an industry that should have been destroyed long ago. He spun stories about the pollutants sent into the ground and the air; that it would be the end of humanity. Before Yun had time to think, he had charged Yun with blowing up the gold mine. After providing all the details even the TNT chemical formula, he promised Yun he would be a hero and that his name would be remembered like his brother's. Yun caught up in Malcolm's world agreed.

As Yun waited for Malcolm's response, he realized he never wanted to blow up the mine. But he had agreed. Guilt brewed inside of him. Everything had been planned and communicated through the game. His game. He waited. His hands were sweating, shaking so he rubbed them hard on his jeans. His fingers still shaking went instinctively to the coin. He closed his eyes and remembered the promise to his brother. The screen remained blank. No response.

He had never felt more alone.

Art stepped into view as soon as Yun began typing again. His squat frame filled the boarding house's tiny doorway leading into the room.

"Contacting your environmental crazies?" Art's voice hit him like a punch in the gut. Yun's chair banged to the floor as he jumped up. He tripped backwards into the wall and made a motion to run around Art. "Take one more step and I'll put a bullet through your skull." Art moved aside his jacket and showed Yun the gun on his waistband.

Yun froze in place. His eyes locked onto the gun in Art's waistband. "I'm n . . .not m... moving." Yun's arms shook as he held them up.

"Just a scientist, huh?" Art closed the small gap between them.

So close that Yun smelled his breath. Stale, rotten, and whiskey. He felt Art's anger emanating from his pores.

Art brought his finger to Yun's chest and pushed him hard into the wall, "That first day you came off the truck there was something nagging me about you. You looked familiar. I decided to do some investigating. And unlucky for you I was a communication expert in security technology." Art's eyes were glazed and unfocused, "I was with the special forces." He paused.

"For the Western Coalition." He moved nose to nose with Yun. "Back in 2034 in China."

Yun sucked in air and nearly collapsed against Art.

Art waited a second and backed up a step, "Yeah, I know all about your activist brother and his group and how they carried out the bombing of the railway in 2034." He tilted his head while his lips broke into a sarcastic grin. "Ya know you two look a lot alike."

"You were there?" Yun managed to whisper.

Art snorted, "I was captured as one of the bombers."

"But. . .but you didn't do it." Yun shook his head.

"Try explaining that to a bunch of blood-thirsty nationalists looking for a scapegoat." When Art moved toward the door, Yun took a quick breath of air thinking perhaps Art would let him go. Afterall, he had nothing to do with what happened in China. Art's hand went to the gun in his waistband. He caressed it. "I was spying for the Western Coalition. They abandoned me when it became a political mess across the globe. They left me in a Chinese prison, but I escaped." His face contorted and he yelled "Ha! I showed them all!" He began mumbling incoherently under his breath and turned his head up toward the sky. From the side Yun could see his jaw relax and his regular scowl left his face. Then just as quickly the scowl returned as he spun to face Yun again, "And looky here! You fall right into my lap in this shithole in the Andes. If I can't get back at the Western Coalition, you'll be a good substitute. It was your brother's fault." Art laughed, "'The sins of the brother'. . . as they say."

"My brother died for his beliefs."

"Yeah. Beliefs. What good are they when you end up tortured and abandoned?" In one swift motion Art yanked Yun's arms around to his back. He then secured them with a wire, tightening it until it broke through Yun's skin leaving drips of red. Art pushed him out of the boarding house and they marched toward the path to the mine.

As Yun trenched across the gravel with Art right behind, the pain in his wrists kept him focused. Yun couldn't believe what he'd heard. How could Art have been there? This was crazy. He always suspected his brother was involved in dangerous activity. And when he found out about the explosion at the railway and how the reports across China decreed Chin a criminal, he knew he must join the group his brother was involved in. The world needed to know his brother wasn't a criminal. He had doubts from the beginning about his brother's connection with *Seeds of Tomorrow* but felt there had to be a way to carry out his brother's vision. A week after the reports of his brother's death had come out, Yun distraught and searching for a way to live a meaningful life, had sought out and joined 'Seeds of Tomorrow'.

But now, Art threatened to derail the plan. A plan that he wasn't so sure anymore should be executed.

THIRTY-SIX

● ●

Mark held his temper when Dr. Davis screamed into his com-chip, "Seriously! Are you telling me all the injections are gone?"

He cleared his throat before responding, "Excuse me, Dr Davis, but we have a critical medical issue happening with your daughter. I'm trying to get her to a hospital in Cusco. She's in a coma." He said this for the third time. He wondered if she had a hearing problem. In the past when he had overheard her talking to Sydney it was always business. Never personal, like a mother would be, never questions like if she's eating right, or about her love life.

Dr. Davis responded, "I'll be in La Rinconada as soon as possible, gather as much physical evidence of this disaster as possible. And keep it all safe." Mark was about to tell her Sydney wouldn't be here by the time she arrived, but the line went dead.

Mark held his hand over his ear where the com-chip was located. He waited until his breathing returned to normal before he pushed to activate, "Darweshi."

"Mark?" Darweshi said.

"Where've you been?"

"I've been in a small empty warehouse at the end of the main road, checking the climate reports. I come here sometimes to get away, have some space."

Mark could hear the anxiety on the other end of the call. Darweshi required direction, someone in control. Sydney was a positive influence for Darweshi and a good leader for them all. But right now, she wasn't here and someone had to keep things going, keep things somewhat normal. He recognized that both Darweshi and he needed something to occupy their minds while Pa'qo was using his skills to help Sydney.

"I'm going to the lab site to pick through the rubble. Dr. Davis wants evidence of what happened with the injections. Meet me there in ten minutes." Mark didn't wait for a reply.

After hanging up from the call, he tried Yun. He didn't get any answer. He peeked into Pa'qo's bedroom. Pa'qo was busy administering to Sydney, who was still unresponsive.

"Can I use your truck?" Mark's heartbeat faster as he looked at Sydney's pale face.

"Yes. Don't worry I will take care of her." Pa'qo didn't move from Sydney's side.

Mark went to Ryan who was balled up in one of Pa'qo's fur blankets lying on the cushions of the chair. He noticed Ryan's breathing was steady. Feeling like there was nothing else for him to do here, Mark left the house, jumped in Pa'qo's truck. It was like being in an old movie from the 90's. He stared at the dash and wondered where the computer was. After a few minutes of total confusion, he noticed the key and turned it. The motor started. He moved a lever to 'D' and pressed the gas pedal.

The only part remaining of the lab was the front wall and part of the side. The rest was a combo of dirt and ice and pieces of wood as well as equipment strewn about against the sheer rock revealed by the landslide. Yun was right about the lab being in a precarious location. Where was Yun? He let that thought go; he'd worry about it later. He concentrated on the search for the injections. It was important, as was the coffee mugs that they both drank from. He was sure when they tested them there would be traces of the poison Art used. Mark was pushing away chunks of dirt and rock when Darweshi arrived.

"Find anything yet?" Darweshi looked around, kicking up gravel and debris where Mark had just moved it.

"We need to get Sydney out of here. I called Puno hospital to get a helicopter to take her to Cusco. But they told me a helicopter can't land here since it can't hover at the elevation in La Rinconada." Mark kicked another bunch of debris. "Damn."

"Do we even know what's wrong with Sydney? What do we say about the CRISPR? What about Art? Is anyone looking for him?" Darweshi grabbed a large piece of lumber. He yanked it and fell onto his back. He stayed there looking up at the sky.

Mark strode over and gave him a hand, "C'mon Dar, don't freak out on me. We need to concentrate on priorities. Keeping Sydney stable while we get her to Puno is number one. The hospital in Puno has a medical team waiting for her. You must be the one to take her there. Do you think you can do that?"

Darweshi stopped brushing off his pants and backed away, "You want me to drive down that suicide path they call a road?"

Mark stepped wrong and turned his ankle over a lab table and winced. "I need you to do this, for Sydney. Because the second priority is to find Art." Mark reached down and pushed the lab table over, unearthing dirt. Amongst a pile of injection needles that were sticking out from a mound of gravel was Sydney's coffee mug. "Yes!", Mark snatched up everything he could and tucked them into a canvas bag. "So, are you going to help or not?" He was getting angry.

"Alright already! I'll get Sydney to Puno. But I may be the one in the hospital."

"I've let the hospital officials know you are coming and gave them a brief about the situation. No telling what kind of mess is going to happen here."

At least he had a plan in place. He would get Sydney safe and with the needed medical attention and then proceed to find Art. Mark and Darweshi hurried back with the evidence to Pa'qo's house to check on Sydney and Ryan.

CHAPTER
THIRTY-SEVEN

The cave had been built centuries ago by the Incas. This specific one was used to store gold icons and relics for the Incan gods. All the treasures were long gone, stolen by Pizarro and other invaders. Yun had spent hours reading about this mine and its history. He wondered how Art discovered it. Doesn't matter. Art now took advantage of the unused vein that led directly to a remote warehouse at the edge of the settlement near his house.

"Well, that's the last of it." Art dropped the container of sulfuric acid inside the abandoned cave. The thump onto the solid dirt reverberated under Yun's body and up through his head. His hands were bound behind his back. His ankles were bound as well. The hazy light coming from the mining lamp cast shadows resembling a two-headed monster with a tiny body. This place was abandoned from the rest of the mining operation. Was this Art's secret hideaway? Yun had researched the mine before arriving in La Rinconada. No one would attempt to come this way. The shafts were unstable. They hadn't been used in a century.

"So that's ten. Should be more than enough to make a giant hole in Katen's operation," Art strode over to where Yun sat against the cave wall.

While Art had been busy with the containers, Yun had twisted the restraints on his legs and hands. He had manipulated them till they were loose. "You had all this stored in the remote warehouse? Why?" Yun hoped to distract Art as he wiggled his fingers behind his back.

"Let's just say I had a profitable business going here but now I'm redirecting myself to the same plan as you and your secret terrorist group, *Seeds of Tomorrow*. Nice game by the way."

Yun shot his head up when Art mentioned the game. He stopped manipulating the ties on his hands.

Art brought his face close to Yun's. "When I breached your game, I discovered that you were planning to blow up this mine." Art waited for Yun to grasp what he just said. "I know all about your plan. And that game you brought was your way to pass information back and forth to your friends. Clever. It tricked everyone else."

He walked back and forth checking each container and removing the top. "I, on the other hand, have much more selfish reasons for blowing up this mine. Nothing so noble as saving the world from environmental disasters. Mine comes from a simple primitive instinct. An eye for an eye. I had a lucrative enterprise going here.

I took advantage of organizations that have a need to destroy. I help them out with their method of eradicating each other, and they help me out financially." Art scoffed as he banged his hand onto the top of one of the containers, "This stuff was banned in 2035 after that railway disaster. They used sulfuric acid to synthesize the explosion. Did you know that? But the stupid government never regulated it. Not my fault if the world's top idiots can't figure out how to control it. And now that scientist of yours ended all my plans by telling Katen."

Yun noticed the containers were placed strategically around the sides of the cave to maximize the explosive potential. Exactly as he would have done if he had the chance to carry out the plan. The unused vein was not structurally secure. If this cave collapsed, the rest of the mine, really the whole side of the glacier, would fail.

"No one will be killed, right?" Yun flipped his hair to cover watery eyes. "Innocent people can't die." He suddenly realized that Chin must've been a little crazy. His brother probably had no reservations about killing people in that railway explosion. But Yun couldn't have innocent people die because of him. He wasn't as much like his brother as he thought.

Art ignored him, "Where did I put the potassium and sugar?" His eyes searched the cave. His eyes glowed revealing how far gone he was. "Amazing, such a simple recipe could cause such a mess. Potassium, a little sugar, mix it all together with sulfuric acid and . . . BOOM!" Art yelled that last word and laughed when Yun cringed. At that same moment a small body propelled itself from a hiding place.

"What? What the hell? How..."

"RYAN," Yun yelled.

Art bolted forward, colliding with Ryan. He grabbed Ryan's shirt and yanked him into a strangle hold. Ryan froze against Art while tears streamed down his face.

"No!" Ryan's strangled cry was barely audible as he looked at Art's arm around his chest.

"Where did he come from?" Art said as he pulled him up into the air leaving the boy's legs dangling.

"I think he was in the shuttle car. I had no idea."

"If he's been hiding there, he knows everything." Art gave Ryan another squeeze.

"What are you going to do? He is just a boy. Please let him go, and I promise the both of us will hide out until you can get away."

"Yeah, right. This doesn't change anything. I simply adjust." Art grunted as he grabbed a piece of rope that was tightly wound to the rail hitch on the shuttle car. He let out a ragged breath.

He tied one end around Ryan's hands and left the other attached to the hitch. Yun's hands were sweaty from manipulating the ties on his wrists, and his pulse quickened from the pain in his head.

"My OID is low." Yun said then he looked at Ryan's arm. He couldn't read Ryan's.

"Dammit," Art mumbled to himself ignoring Yun. He tapped the face of his own OID device watching the readout. "No wonder I'm out of breath." Art took a quick look at them, "Don't do anything stupid."

Yun watched Art pound away through the darkness. Yun huddled against the crumbling wet earth devising an escape.

CHAPTER
THIRTY-EIGHT

When Mark and Darweshi returned, Pa'qo could hardly get the words out, "Your. . . Ryan. . . ran." Pa'qo placed a hand on Mark's arm. "I was tending to Sydney. Ryan was gone when I came to him."

Mark's forehead creased as the words penetrated. He clenched Pa'qo's hand that was still on his arm. "Ryan?" Without another word he spun from Pa'qo and burst back through the door. He blinked his eyes to hold back the anger and tears. He needed to think clearly. His son was alone, out of his element. Who knows what he would do? He had to find him now. The pond! He raced to the same path that led to the pond where Ryan went when he ran away from the lab. His mind pushed out everything but his son. He didn't feel the cold air assaulting every one of his senses. His son would want to go to a place he associated with calmness.

It was a starry night and the moon shone on the glacier illuminating the path. Mark tilted his head to look up at La Bella Durmiente. A ring of icy light surrounded the peak. He heard animals growling and turned in a circle trying to locate where the sounds were coming from. He'd never seen the pumas but listened to them in the dark hours when he couldn't sleep. He'd become familiar with the low extended growl that rose from the back of their throats. They were night hunters who stalked their prey. They typically went for small mammals. Nearly extinct, the remaining few only existed here, in La Rinconada. Mark was sure the dead puma Ryan and Pa'qo had discovered was the result of Art poisoning one of them. The man was mad and calculating.

Mark stood where he first met Pa'qo that day at the edge of the pool. This was a special place for Ryan. He listened for the cats again and called out Ryan's name.

The bushes rustled along the edge of the pond across from where he stood. "Stand where you are." He recognized Art's gravelly voice.

Mark rushed toward the voice. "Where's my son?"

Art slithered out. Mark ignored the gun in his hand and grabbed Art's shirt. His anger pulsated through his whole body as they stood eye to eye. "We've got you, you bastard. We got evidence. Now, take me to my son." Mark spat out the words. Art had Ryan. He felt it in his bones.

"What makes you think you can give me orders?" Art pushed him away and shook the gun loosely back and forth. "Doesn't matter now anyway, everything is gonna be blown away. The gold mine will be a massive hole with Yun buried in it. And that little brat of yours can't keep himself out of trouble. I'm gonna . . ."

Mark lunged, landing a solid head-butt into his chest. The pain from the impact rippled down Mark's spine. Still groggy from the poison, Mark forced himself to stand straight. Art had tipped back from the force of the blow and dropped the gun. For a few seconds Mark's eyes focused on where the gun had fallen. Art charged.

Soft flesh met up with hard knuckles. Mark heard the crunch in his jaw before feeling the pain. For a stocky man Art was fast. He had spun around after delivering the punch and grabbed Mark from the back in a strangle hold. Mark shoved his forearm up to block Art's arm from cinching around his neck. But he was too slow. He couldn't shake the sluggishness that clouded his senses. Art's bulging arm squeezed even tighter blocking his airflow. Marks' eyes blurred and his body twitched. He pictured Ryan calling out for him. Art shifted his weight and the constriction around his neck slackened, allowing a breath to fill his lungs. Mark kicked with all his strength backwards landing his foot on Art's knee cap. Art yelled but didn't let go. He threw his right arm around Mark's neck, now crimping him with both arms in a headlock. Mark was prepared this time. He tightened the muscles in his neck. He visualized where the gun had fallen and judged the distance. He jerked using the force of his whole body and flipped forward toward the ravine sending them both on the ground, hard as cement. Mark grunted as he stretched his fingers out from his knuckles to grab the gun. He found the metal handle and started to raise his arm just as Art pushed up to his feet and kicked Mark's arm. The gun jolted from his hand and disappeared in the dark. Mark grabbed Art's foot and twisted. Art tripped backwards and managed to stay on his feet a few yards away from the edge of the ravine. Mark jumped up and propelled himself toward Art. Art stepped aside and threw out his leg just as Mark got to him. Mark swore as he tumbled headfirst over rock and gravel into the ravine.

CHAPTER
THIRTY-NINE

"She will not live if you take her from here," Pa'qo said.

Sydney's eyes fluttered open when she heard Pa'qo. She could feel Darweshi moving her onto a soft, warm cover and then wrapping her body like a cocoon. This all felt calming until her breath was knocked out of her as Darweshi lifted her and slung her like a sack over his shoulder.

"Mark gave me orders to have Sydney taken to Puno. The truck is waiting outside." Darweshi said.

"I'm not going anywhere!" Sydney interrupted him with a croak. Her throat was scratchy, and her voice barely audible.

Stunned, Darweshi spun in a circle. Sydney tensed struggling inside the blanket prison.

Pa'qo stopped Darweshi and guided him to sit on the bed rolling Sydney back onto the mattress. "Listen. Her breathing." Pa'qo held his hand near her face. "She is back."

"Yes! I am!" She was sure she screamed. But only a slight sound erupted from her mouth. She fought with the blanket getting her feet caught as she tried to get up. "Sydney, are you okay?" Darweshi almost fell on top of her trying to give her a hug.

"Get me out of this!" She pulled herself free.

Pa'qo immediately pulled out his medicines and concocted a mixture from several different colored bottles. "I will make sure your body and mind are healed. Please take this?" Pa'qo held a small vial of murky brown fluid for her to take.

He guided the vial from his hand to hers. She calmed down and drank the liquid amazed at how much she trusted him. She handed the empty vial back to Pa'qo and turned toward the bedroom window where a foggy mist had formed over the glacier.

"Where's Ryan . . . and Mark?" She managed after swallowing the warm liquid. "

Mark is out looking for Ryan. . . who ran away." Darweshi looked out the window, squeezing his hands together.

"Why aren't you helping him!" Sydney searched the room trying to get her bearings back. Her body was weak, but her voice got stronger.

"She's right." Pa'qo put his hand on Darweshi's arm, "Mark has been gone too long. Ryan is in danger. I feel it. You must go."

"You're scaring me with all this." Darweshi put his hands up in protest and backed away.

"Go to the pond where Ryan ran that day." Pa'qo's voice filled the room commanding Darweshi.

"He's a young, scared boy. You must go or I will!" Sydney was about to break apart.

Everything that happened here was her fault.

Darweshi tucked his chin and finally nodded. He took off for the pond without another word. Sydney wobbled over to Pa'qo rubbing her forehead. The pain was making it difficult to see.

"Do you know why we came here? To La Rinconada?" Now engaged in this mess, Sydney needed to give him an explanation. She searched Pa'qo's face for any hints of anger. She wouldn't blame him if he was angry with all of them. With her.

"Ah. You must not let the worry of what I think bother you. I have known for many years about man using ego to explain the hurt they inflict on earth. Our Mother has been speaking and I have seen how she has suffered. Men with little connection to Pachamama can't see past the next day. But I have seen."

"But do you know that earth's atmosphere will not have enough oxygen for humans to exist? That everyone will die? We have a plan to stop that from happening. That's what we are trying to do here. To save humankind." She needed him to understand.

"I am aware of the devastation that lurks. I had a talk with Mark. While he did not reveal any details, I could read what was happening. My people have long been angry at your people's lack of ability to live as one with nature. Yet now I see you are doing what you believe is right and doing it with goodness in your heart. That is all I need to know. I will help. Pachamama will help."

At that moment Sydney could see that Pa'qo and his people were more aligned with the 'Protect and Respect' engraving over the Institute's entrance than any one of them. Her discussion with Azucena came back in a wave. Their connection to the earth. These people knew how to protect and respect the earth. They lived it every day. And Pa'qo was their leader.

She was in the presence of a humble, great man. There was no room for arrogance or pride in this man's world.

CHAPTER
FORTY

The pain in Yun's hands had weakened him. He could barely think, yet he fought. He kept prying his fingers around the wire. His fingers were flexible, thanks to all the game playing. Ryan remained tied to the rail of the shuttle car and watched.

"I'll get you out of here. I almost got it."

"I heard everything. You are bad too."

"Sometimes the definition of who is bad can be relative. I know I did what most consider terrible things - being involved with people who blew up places. . . but I never wanted to hurt people. The reason was to have a future for you, for all generations to come." The wire around his wrists came loose and Yun slipped his hands free. He rubbed the blood off and went to work on releasing the ropes around his ankles. He blew out a sigh. "I'm still committed to that purpose." He tried to stand and fell over. His legs were weak. He crawled over to Ryan.

"I thought you were my friend?" Ryan pushed his back against the metal rail to get away from Yun.

"I am." Yun took hold of Ryan's rope and yanked it loose. Ryan shimmied out from its coil, and quickly tripped away from Yun.

"I hope your life will be good, Ryan. All I wanted was to make a difference in this world. To carry on where my brother left off." Yun stood up and limped over to the containers. "Even if my methods were misguided."

Ryan looked at Yun surrounded by the containers against the cave wall then tore away and ran out of the mine.

Yun lost no time. He stared at the materials for the explosion. All week he'd been thinking about his brother. Chin was the natural leader when they were children living in their small village by the Yangtze. As a young child Yun recognized that gift. He had come to recognize that Chin was unstable and that, unfortunately, was part of his allure. The children of the village would follow him on whatever mission he devised. When those simple playful missions became first dangerous and then illegal, it was too late. Yun loved his brother knowing in the back of his mind that one day Chin would go too far. And now he was ready to do what he must, what he promised. . . for Chin. His only hope was that Art would be with him at the end when the mountain collapsed. Yun turned toward the explosives.

CHAPTER
FORTY-ONE

M ark found himself face down in a pool of muck at the bottom of a pit. He pulled himself up, all limbs functional, but the mud mixed with the gravel and the slant of the slope made it impossible to get a footing. He looked around for pieces of wood or trees that he could pile and climb to reach the top. There was nothing but dirt in this hole, with no way out. He sat down in the cold dirt and forced his thoughts to focus on a way out. Precious seconds were ticking away. He heard a rumbling. He listened. It was Pa'qo's truck. He could tell by the way it kept backfiring. "Help! I'm in the ravine. HELP!"

The engine stopped, "Mark? Mark, where are you?" Seconds later Mark saw the flashlight skimming the surface of the ravine floor.

"Here, over here."

"Are you hurt?" Darweshi called as the light flooded Mark face.

"No. Just hurry up and get me out of here. Art has Ryan somewhere in the mine."

"I'll get the rope from the truck."

Climbing up the side while attached to a rope wasn't easy—more like three steps forward and then a backslide—but at least the backslides didn't land him back at the bottom. Mark was operating on pure adrenaline. Soon, he and Darweshi were speeding across the bumpy landscape as the truck carried them toward the entrance to the mine. Mark drove careening on two wheels around the last corner when the sign for the entrance came in sight.

Then it was gone. A deafening explosion shook the side of the mountain while smoke and debris obliterated the entrance. A shock wave thrust the truck backwards. It was impossible to see through the haze of the explosion's aftermath. Mark used all his strength to gain control of the steering wheel and made a sharp left off the road. He barely missed a boulder as the truck came to an abrupt halt tilting against it. Darweshi jumped out of the vehicle.

"What the hell was that?" Darweshi said. Mark dashed off toward the entrance.

Mark coughed and shielded his eyes with his hand to keep the dust from blinding him. He could see some semblance of the entrance but there was too much rock and dirt. He took a flashlight from his back pocket. Darweshi scurried from behind, huffing out of breath.

"What do you think happened?" Darweshi gasped between deep inhales.

"I don't care about that right now. Right now, all I want is my son."

Mark cast the flashlight over the mounds of rock and dirt but it did no good; the dust reflected the light back. He turned it off, feeling for a way forward—and heard coughing. Ryan tripped out of the darkness and plowed into his father's arms.

Mark took the full force against him.

"Dad, Dad, Dad," Ryan couldn't stop yelling.

"Thank God." Mark embraced him. He squeezed him so tight that Ryan started squirming. Mark held onto his son's shoulders at arms-length examining his face and body. "Are you hurt?"

"No. Not hurt. Yun sent me out before he made the explosion."

"Yun's in there?" Darweshi said.

"I've got to get him out." Mark said, "Ryan stay here with Dar." He turned searching where Ryan had exited. There were rocks, dust, and piles of debris everywhere.

Ryan put his face against his father's leg and wrapped his arms around him. "No, no. He did it on purpose. He was on a mission." He started to cry.

Mark stood with Ryan, staring at the destroyed mine whilst his son blurted out a confused story. If he understood Ryan correctly, it was Yun's desire to die.

They all went back to the truck with Mark carrying Ryan in his arms. He settled Ryan in the front seat before he and Darweshi rocked the vehicle back and forth until it was off the boulder and onto the road. Darweshi drove leaving the dark and dust from the mountain behind them.

Pressed between Darweshi and his father, Ryan wouldn't stop talking, starting from when he ran from Pa'qo's house to when Yun released him from the ropes. Ryan explained that he had been scared and wanted to help his dad. That's why he ran. He was looking for Mark.

Mark shook his head and squeezed him tighter to his side, "You're safe now."

Mark couldn't quite understand why Yun blew up the mine. But one thing he was clear about. Nobody harms his son. He had an inkling of where Art was going next. Pa'qo's house. He needed to get to the evidence he'd left there.

CHAPTER
FORTY-TWO

h-ODD 7955
Oxygen level 20.3

Sydney's whole body ached like she had run a marathon in a desert. Her head spun. Her mouth was dry and her eyes blurry. She tried to get her bearings as Pa'qo's calming hands hovered over her head as he prayed. The sound of his voice brought her to a calm place, and she swore she felt a warmness flowing through her.

"The medicine I gave can take time. You must not get up. You need to gather strength."

She pushed herself halfway up. "There's too much I must do. How long was I unconscious?" As the words came out of her mouth, a blast rocked the bed and thrust her body back down. "What was that?" Her face tightened and her body stiffened. She twisted her body to look at Pa'qo. "It sounded like an explosion."

He took her hand, "The world is changing and Pacha-mama is purging evil from the mountain." For a second, she thought he knew what was going to happen before it did. Pa'qo held her hand and gazed into the night like he was seeing something. "Art is planning death.

The spirits have long abandoned him."

She scrunched her forehead and let go of his hand, "Art is mad. He's dangerous. He's the root of all this." Sydney needed to fix all this. She needed to do something.

Pa'qo kept silent.

"Pa'qo, I have to get up."

"I gave you quechua medicine. Your body needs rest and healing time. I will go and calm the people. They will be huddled together in their homes. They will need me to guide them from this darkness."

"And I need to get a new project going. Were there any injections left?"

"All injections were destroyed in the landslide." Pa'qo gently pressed her back down on the bed.

"And Mark went to find Ryan? Did they come back yet?" Her mind was a jumble. She had lost track of time.

"Not yet."

She held her hands to her temple. "Why can't I focus!" She put her face in her hands. A throbbing migraine threatened her resolve. From years of practice, she forced her thoughts to concentrate on what needed to be done.

Before she put words to her thoughts Pa'qo spoke. "My people will help. You do not need to take on all this by yourself."

"But your people may be in danger too. I couldn't live with the knowledge that something happened to them. We brought so much turmoil with us. You must make sure they are safe. I know I've asked so much from you and your people already but I can't stop thinking about Ryan. Do you think you can ask for help after seeing to their safety? She stared at Pa'qo - as he nodded.

After a long, ragged breath, "I'll stay here and call Dr. Davis. Tell her to bring the authorities. Maybe you can get someone to get us down this mountain." She scrambled from the bed, "I have some of my notes in my room. If I can collect them, get to another lab, somewhere close, maybe Cuzco, I can redo the edit and only be a few days behind on the plan. I'll tell Dr. Davis to set up a lab there."

One minute, Pa'qo faced Sydney, the next, he collapsed to the floor. Standing in his place was Art. She saw the burning hatred in his eyes, his whole face red. She looked down at the gun in his hand. He had knocked Pa'qo out with the handle. Art took a step over Pa'qo's body. She felt her blood pulsating through her veins as she fell to her knees beside Pa'qo, "What are you doing?" She couldn't look at Art. She felt Pa'qo's chest, the pulse in his neck.

"I need that evidence." He stood over them.

"What evidence?"

"That mug."

"What mug?" She found a pulse. "Were you responsible for that explosion?" Sydney's voice shook but she tried to remain calm.

Art stomped past Sydney and threw open cabinets and drawers, becoming increasingly frantic. He tipped over Pa'qo's lab table, spilling medicines and herbs, finally resorting to kicking anything that was in his way. "I'll find it. Yun is dead, by the way, in the explosion you heard.

And you might as well give up on Mark. Right now, he's kissing the bottom of a ravine."

"What did you do? What do you mean Yun's dead?" She couldn't process what he told her. She cradled Pa'qo's head and quietly breathed relief as his eyes blinked open.

"So much you don't know for being a brilliant scientist," a corner of Art's mouth lifted in a smirk. He searched the mess in the room and grunted with sick amusement when he uncovered the coffee mug and a small vile lying on the floor next to the bed. "Yes, Yun. It was his plan to blow up the mine. And that kid, Ryan? He was just in the wrong place at the wrong time."

Her scream exploded inside her head No,no,no!

Tucking the coffee mug inside his coat, he stood at the back doorway and leveled the gun at her. "I'm outta here. But not before I finish some business." The snake was barring its fangs as she stared up at the gun. Pa'qo moved to stand.

A small figure burst through the front room and landed on top of her, "Sydney!"

At the same time a blast reverberated around the small room, and she felt Pa'qo roll on top of her and Ryan with him.

Mark and Darweshi exploded through the front door. She couldn't move. Ryan was still on top of her. Pa'qo groaned beside them. Mark dropped next to Sydney and Ryan.

Darweshi yelled, "Pa'qo's bleeding."

Mark ran his hands over Ryan as his eyes searched Sydney's face.

"I wasn't hit. It's Pa'qo. Help Pa'qo." She tried to get up. "Art! Where'd he go? Did you see him? He came searching for evidence and couldn't miss a second chance to get rid of me. Pa'qo saved us."

"I'll find him." Mark's voice shook everything in the tiny room. She could feel the heat from his anger.

"There." Pa'qo motioned with his hand toward the back of the house.

Before she had time to think Mark raced out the back following Art's trail. Ryan jumped to go after his father. Sydney grabbed his small shaking body and held him tight. "I promise your dad will be okay. I promise." She didn't know how.

Darweshi went to Pa'qo who was pale. He checked his breathing and the wound. "Looks like the bullet went straight through. We need to stop the bleeding."

"Use that." Sydney pointed at the sheet from the bed.

Darweshi tore it in strips and wrapped it around Pa'qo's wound. Ryan remained against Sydney and raised his eyes to Pa'qo.

"I am fine, Ryan. I am now bandaged and there is no more blood," Pa'qo lifted his hand toward an old cabinet against the wall. It looked Spanish in origin, with intricate black wood scrollwork and painted scenes on the doors depicting royalty from an ancient time. "It is time for the end of this. You must confront this evil that invaded our lives. Open the cabinet."

Sydney wasn't sure she heard him, "What do you mean, *you* must confront? And how's something in that old cabinet going to help?"

"There is a powerful relic inside wrapped in blue cloth."

Sydney hesitated. She'd question him later about her role in 'confronting this evil'. Right now, her curiosity got the best of her. She unwrapped her arms from Ryan and went to the cabinet. The handle of the door was a pulley made of some old metal, maybe iron. She carefully tugged it. It didn't budge. She sighed and yanked it harder. It clicked. Inside, all the way to the back, behind different odd-shaped bottles and stacked notebooks that looked like they'd crumble if disturbed, was something wrapped in ice-blue silk. Before even touching the silk, she got a whiff of a musty aroma. When was the last time this cabinet had been opened? She raised her gaze to Pa'qo. He nodded. She reached in. It was heavy in her hand as she took it from its resting place. As her fingers worked to unfold the corners dust rose to her face. She squinted her eyes shut and opened them. A knife. The blade was about 6" long but it was the handle that she couldn't take her eyes from.

Darweshi's fingers reached for it. "Are those stones real?"

Pa'qo settled on the chair holding his injured shoulder. "Every shaman since the ancient times has preserved the knife, keeping it safe before passing it to the next generation of shamans. It was bloodied only once to defend the last Sapa Inca, Atahualpa, 500 years ago."

Sydney's hand trembled almost dropping the relic. She held it out to Pa'qo. "I can't handle this. It's too precious."

Pa'qo went to Sydney and held his hands over hers as she tried to give him the knife. He continued speaking while his hands hovered over hers, "It is written in the scrolls from long ago that the knife was used by the imperial bodyguard protecting Atahualpa before he was executed by Pizarro." His chest heaved and he coughed. His face scrunched in pain and he grabbed hold of her arm that held the knife.

"Pa'qo!" Sydney's attention turned from the knife to Pa'qo. She didn't know how much more he could take. The white sheet turned red around the wound.

He shook his head and let go of her arm. His voice grew stronger, "The Incas believe each Sapa was the son of the Incan Sun god and that Atahualpa will return for this knife to restore the people to majesty and peace."

Pa'qo's face was pale even though he sounded stronger. Sydney shook her head, "But Art has a gun."

"The knife will protect you." Pa'qo closed his eyes and recited a chant. A vibration almost like a purring sound emanated from his throat. This was very different to the other prayers she'd heard from him.

As Pa'qo chanted, Ryan ran to Sydney. Despite the turmoil of what had transpired, she forced herself to remain calm. He embraced her from behind. She felt his body relax into her. She looked down at the knife and knew that as crazy as this all seemed, she had to do something. What chance did Mark really have against a gun, not that she had much more chance with a knife but at least it was something. That's what Pa'qo meant about confronting the evil. She felt Ryan's embrace tighten. How would she ever forgive herself for allowing Ryan to come with them? She placed the knife carefully on Pa'qo's worktable, turned and stooped down to face him. Her arms encircled his slight body, and something fluttered in her chest that she never had felt before.

"Are you going after him?" Darweshi's shaky voice brought her back. He had been witnessing all of it from the corner of the room.

Darweshi couldn't do what needed to be done. She couldn't pawn this off to anyone else. Sydney took Ryan's hand and led him to Pa'qo. She resolved to get this over with. She went back to the table and took the knife into her hand. It felt soothing and warm yet a strange chill ran through her body. This was just a knife. How was it going to protect her? She was still weak from the poison. Two amber stones shone with an inner fire; they glowed with a life of their own. Small green gems surrounded each amber jewel. The gems were embedded in a bone handle and the blade had strange markings etched on one side. Pa'qo stood and leaned against the cabinet. He clenched his jaw. Sweat beaded his forehead.

"You need medical attention."

At her words, Pa'qo straightened. His eyes focused on her. "Go. Atahualpa will be with you."

"I'm thinking this isn't a good idea." Darweshi moved over to Pa'qo who held Ryan's hand.

"I know," Sydney took in the three of them. Looking at Ryan sealed her decision. Maybe she'd find Mark and they'd both go after Art. "I will do this." Her words sounded strange to her ears. The adrenaline pumped through her body. "He won't get away with what he did." She left in the direction of Art's house. If he was planning on disappearing, he needed to collect some belongings. It was almost dawn. The temperature was just above freezing yet she felt only a warm tingle inside her belly. The grey cast from the sky turned a little less dark. She kept her eyes focused on the dirt road as she wound around the town and came upon a narrow path that directed her straight to Art's house. In the distance she was sure she heard low growls. Probably the pumas. When she got there the first thing that came to her mind was how tiny the house was. It was built next to a slightly larger ramshackle wooden structure erected against the side of the mine. Beyond that was barren tundra as far as the eye could see. The exhaustion from the past twenty-four hours threatened to overwhelm her. Her breathing ragged, she blinked twice to focus and studied her OID to make sure she had enough oxygen. Again, a deadly reminder of why they were here. *This* is why they had come all the way to La Rinconada. She had to keep going. People . . .everyone, in every corner of the earth, would be impacted if they didn't succeed. She wasn't alone. She had Pa'qo, whom she now considered a friend and all the people living here in this remote part of the planet who had so much to offer the world: their culture and their beliefs. In the span of one week there was so much that had happened. Tears formed as she thought of Yun, a young man at the beginning of his life who didn't deserve to die. She shook off the thought. She had to stay clear-headed. She trudged along toward the back of the house trying to conserve energy and pump up her spirit. Her mind went to Darweshi. He was a loyal and good friend. He would follow her anywhere even if it terrified him. Her face relaxed. And although initially vexed by Mark's continued attention she was beginning to realize the strength she felt from him. His strength fed hers. Feelings were growing and she felt her body respond with the thought of him. Everything else she ever did, her purpose in life could never compare to her purpose right now. An invisible force propelled her forward. The force had a face. Ryan's. She was doing this for him.

"Stop right there," A voice bellowed disrupting Sydney's thoughts.

She fell to the ground digging her nails into the gravel. She waited. She had to find shelter. Turning her head slightly from left to right she spotted a small mound not far from where she was. She slithered like a snake till she was shielded by the dirt mound. Her heart pounded against her chest. Nothing happened. It was Art's voice. Where was he? She tilted her ear trying to key on where his voice had come from. She peeked above the top of the mound.

He wasn't anywhere. But she did see someone else.

Mark stood in profile staring ahead. He lifted his face. He stood stiff, unmoving. His face glistened with the morning mist. The sun was rising and in seconds would shine directly at him.

It was then that she noticed the figure in the shadows. She couldn't see him but knew it was Art. She froze. He had addressed Mark not her.

"It's time for you to stop this madness." Mark shouted toward the shadow. He looked ready to pounce. He moved a step closer keeping his eyes focused on Art. The gravel under his foot crunched.

"I said stop! What do you think you're gonna do? Use some stupid scientific reasons with words about a better tomorrow? Ha!" Art shifted his weight. "But you're right. It's time to end this whole thing, right here, right now." He raised his gun, aiming directly at Mark.

The sun blazed across the horizon. Light flooded everywhere illuminating the ice and treeless landscape. Mark lifted his hand to block the brilliance. Suddenly Sydney's body was no longer her own. Her fears were replaced with a total disregard for her own safety as she jumped from her hiding place clenching the knife. She ran forward, positioning her body between Mark and Art and raised the knife over her head bracing for the attack. The sun bounced off the gems in the handle and onto Art's face. As the path of the burning light continued to burst over the horizon, hitting its mark, Art's features became a grotesque scowl. He turned his head away. The angry roar of a wild animal froze Sydney in her place. The sound echoed into the void. Three pumas charged from behind Art's house. The largest, with a dark black spot between her eyes, leaped toward Art's arm that held the gun. Another cat opened its jaw to strike at his neck.

A shot shuddered against the mountain. The one going for his neck collapsed to the ground bleeding. The large female let out what sounded like a painful shriek and with a vicious protective instinct buried in all creatures, sunk her teeth into Art's forearm. From Art's throat came an unearthly noise. He dropped the gun as the cat released his arm. The scream he released told of the pain that must have flooded every fiber of his being. Holding his arm, he crawled into the building against the mountain. Sydney did not dare move. Where was Mark? She held her breath and out of the corner of her eye she watched the third cat disappear heading in the opposite direction of Art. A growl brought her focus back. The female remained with pieces of Art's shirt hanging from her bloodied mouth. She sniffed the dead cat lying on the barren ground then slowly twisted her head and captured Sydney's eyes. Sydney stood, spellbound. This was it. There was no way she could outrun an animal so wild and powerful. This was how she was going to die. The eyes of the cat bore into her, and Sydney felt a presence. It was a life-force beyond the body of the animal. Then she noticed that their eyes were amber, same as the gems in the knife still clenched in her hand. The cat blinked and the presence vanished. The animal turned and broke into a run.

CHAPTER
FORTY-THREE

* * *

h-ODD 10,005
Oxygen level 20.2

The next day Sydney greeted five of Katen's security men who arrived with their own vehicles and by late afternoon La Rinconada teemed with local police from Puno. The van that had broken down was fixed and explained away as an accident attributed to the typical rockslides on the dangerous mountain road. The confrontation on the mountain with Art and the pumas however couldn't be explained, no matter how she tried to make sense of the incident. It was a feeling with no scientific support. Was she ready to consider other explanations? Earlier that morning she had arrived at Pa'qo's to return the knife and see if he had any information that would give her some reason for what she experienced.

He was nowhere to be found. She wrapped the knife in the blue cloth and returned it to its safe place in the cabinet with a note on his worktable to contact her asap. Last night all Mark could tell her was he saw a flash of light, followed by a scream. He swore he didn't see her until it was over. He had told her one minute he was facing a gun barrel and then next she was standing in front of him with a knife yelling his name. Nothing about the pumas. She had questioned him again this morning. He had the same story. She watched him now as the police listened to his story about the explosion and what happened to Yun. She overheard that they wanted to talk to Ryan. Mark shook his head. "Right now, I'll help you find Art Saunders. We'll discuss questioning Ryan later". With that he took off with the police leading them on the path to Art's house.

Sydney went in the opposite direction and headed towards the spot with the

'Bienvenidos La Rinconada' sign behind her. The same spot she had stood when she first arrived in La Rinconada. A wave of belonging, of feeling connected to the land and the people washed over her. So much had happened. Darweshi, Ryan and Pa'qo were already there when she arrived. She made a mental note to speak with Pa'qo later about the knife. They all watched the truck drive up the path. The volunteers were coming in the next truck. This one was filled with the team of her mother's hand-picked scientists. This promised to be an interesting 'catch-up' meeting. The desolate, barren landscape greeted the visiting scientists as they exited the vehicle with slow careful movements. Sydney couldn't believe her eyes. She couldn't remember the last time she had seen Aunt Rene.

An all too familiar command hijacked the swift sweet memory, "What's happened here?" Dr. Davis was the first one who hopped out and hit the gravel hard with her feet. In her usual manner, she addressed Sydney without any preamble. "You better have some solid explanation for holding up the original plan. Even if the edits were destroyed, as you say."

Dr. Davis had cut her grey-streaked hair short, which made her tall lanky frame more intimidating. Her face showed no expression as she paced in front of Sydney as if she was in an auditorium with an audience. "The gene edit was the agreed-upon plan. It has a proven track record with directing the significant changes in the body. As of now, my team will take over your project. The international—"

"Mother—"

"—community—"

"Mother!"

The sound of gravel crunching stopped as Dr. Davis spun around. Sydney walked up to her and touched her mother's shoulder, "I'm happy you came," With all that had happened over the past week she welcomed the familiar dissonance of their relationship.

"Well, well, um," her mother seemed shaken by her daughter's touch but remained stiff, "and how. . ."

"I'm fine." Sydney responded to the half-asked question. "Please give me a minute to explain what has happened here."

As Sydney outlined the details, Davis remained uncharacteristically quiet. She could see in her mother's hard-lined forehead that her mind was in overdrive. She ignored her mother's shaking head when she got to the part of how she was treated by Pa'qo and his ancient remedies. Only when she talked about Ryan and the explosion in the mine did her voice falter and she noticed some emotion in her mother's face. She relayed the incident with Art shooting Pa'qo and her voice quickened describing the encounter with the pumas. She purposefully omitted how the incident with the pumas left her with a strange sensation. Sydney was still coming to terms with the confrontation.

Sydney was not just explaining to her mother. She turned realizing everyone had been listening to her description of the events. She caught Aunt Rene's gaze and felt the strength from the love and support that was always there. Her voice became loud, "I believe there is more to be found here, in this ancient place. More in terms of a valuable connection between biology and botany." She knew her mother couldn't dismiss this since she founded the Institute on that very connection between earth and man. If Dr. Davis contradicted her, it would be seen as a contradiction of everything her mother was known for in the world. "Dr. DeSalvo, you must see the possibility in what I've described?"

Before Aunt Rene could respond Dr. Davis addressed the team, "I need to speak with my daughter alone." Her voice suspended any further conversation. "All of you, go to your rooms, get settled, and wait for my call." Dr. DeSalvo nodded to Dr. Davis and directed a slight smile at Sydney. The other scientists, all too familiar with her mother's abruptness, left without a word.

Sydney nudged Darweshi as he put his hand on Ryan's shoulder to lead him away. Pa'qo quietly disappeared.

Dr. Davis' face relaxed as she watched Aunt Rene walk toward the boarding house.

"What is it, mother?"

Dr. Davis shook her head, "I need to tell you something before we go any further. It's high time you knew about some things in your life and about Rene. Believe it or not, I see how you still connect with her even after all these years. This project is too critical to have you distracted and I need to get you back on track. We may as well lay all the cards on the table. I've had this on my mind since you left for La Rinconada."

Sydney waited and watched as her mother marched down the dirt road speaking, "You remind me of Rene when we were both young. All this talk of connections and ancient cures."

"Mother, stop. What is it? What do you need to tell me?" Sydney took two long strides to catch up. Walking side by side, she decided on a different tactic, "Listen, I'm exhausted, and I'm sure you are as well. I'm certainly not myself right now."

"Yes, whatever that is." Dr. Davis stopped walking, "You know you're not like your father and heaven knows you certainly are not like me."

"What?"

"Can we find a place to sit and talk for a minute?" Dr. Davis exhaled heavily. Sydney slowed down her pace. "Of course."

When they got to the boarding house, Sydney asked Azucena if she would mind bringing two cups of hot tea. The kind woman had offered tea each evening when Sydney dragged herself back from the lab. There was such a sense of community here, of helping each other.

Azucena nodded at the request and slipped away.

Dr. Davis situated herself on the only chair in Sydney's room. Sydney sat on her bed facing her, waiting.

Her mother blew out a sigh as if preparing herself for a difficult discussion. "I wanted so much. I wanted the best education for you, have you part of the most prestigious science network around the globe. Your father was a hard man and certainly not a good father. But he was, or rather is, a brilliant scientist. We always knew he would make some phenomenal discovery one day. But with all that brilliance, there are downsides. He had tunnel vision. He was only able to concentrate on his own agenda." Davis avoided Sydney's eyes. Sydney felt the trepidation. She wondered if she should reach out. But just as she lifted her hand Davis continued. "I was at the hospital one night. When I returned to our apartment he was gone. I was frantic. He later said he had needed to pick up some papers from the lab and had left you alone in your crib. That it would've only taken twenty minutes. You were only a year old. I was so shaken when I came home that night and found you alone. I couldn't hold back. I packed all our things and left him the next day."

Sydney had never heard this story. When very young she'd asked why she didn't have a father. Her mother simply said he valued his career over family and left. No other explanation was ever given. "So, he felt nothing for me?"

"I don't know, he certainly didn't prioritize you. I should've guessed he'd be like that, after all he was never able to give attention, or any form of affection to me. Unfortunately, in a way, I ended up doing the same thing to you. I was so angry at him. I felt he made me leave him. That he forced my hand. I wanted to show him that I could do both even if he couldn't. But I didn't consider how much effort it was to raise a child alone and concentrated on my vision of a career. As you got older, I chose my career. I rationalized that you would be able to deal with having absent parents. That you would be fine without all the silly childhood trappings of birthday parties and sleepovers. I became like your father; I dedicated my life to my work and just assumed you would figure things out for yourself." Dr. Davis rubbed her forehead with her fingers.

Sydney broke the silence, "I see."

There was a soft knock at the door. Azucena brought in their tea and set it on the small end table. "Thank you." The door clicked shut. Sydney felt the sting of salt from the tears pooling but not yet falling. The non-feeling way her mother described how she had dismissed a child for a career almost broke her in two. Somehow, she had always reasoned there was some external force that kept her mother from being a loving parent. That perhaps her mother even had a chemical imbalance that caused her cold behavior. She remembered making up stories when she was lonely and trying to deal with it all. Then Aunt Rene came into her life. The person who had never let her down. She took a long breath. Her sadness turned to resignation. "I see you are right about some things. I am nothing like you and nothing like my father.

I care for people and would never do that to a child. Thank God I had Aunt Rene."

Davis stood up, took a few steps around the room, then turned and sat down again,

"That's the thing I need to tell you. Rene and I were lovers after your father left."

"What?" Sydney's head jerked up. Her teacup shattered on the floor as she sprung up from the bed. They both watched as the scalding liquid seeped through the wood planks.

"I never loved your father. It was always Rene."

"Is that why she was around for most of my childhood?"

Her mother shifted her feet away from the spreading liquid. "Rene told me a long time ago she wanted to spend time with you. That she enjoyed watching you grow." She glanced at her clothes and brushed a non-existent piece of lint from her pants. "She would have been happy to be part of your life even if she and I had nothing between us. I think Rene sensed that I was not the motherly type and easily stepped into that role. I encouraged it since I was never going to be that person for you."

Sydney shook her head, staring at the wet floor. The insensitivity of her mother encouraging someone else to play that role hit a nerve. Her hands shook as she bent to gather the broken pieces of the cup. She looked up at her mother not knowing what to say.

"If you're interested, we're still together, after all these years." Her mother stood and walked across the plank floor toward the door.

Her emotions were jumbled. She decided she wouldn't give her mother anything, "It's really none of my business."

The small room got silent. Sydney continued to pick up the broken pieces of cup. Like my life, she thought. I'm always left picking up pieces and putting them back together. There was nothing else to say. Sydney caught the look of relief on her mother's face as she shut the door. That revelation wasn't for Sydney's benefit. The air of the cold room descended like a heavy weight. Finally, the tears trickled down her cheek. An image of Aunt Rene took shape, a memory of a quiet intelligent person who showed up in her life, shaping her life. Memories flooded in. Like when she had lost the science fair to a rival, Joey Rivera, when she was ten years old. Mother admonished her for choking at the last minute, for not being more aggressive with her final speech to the judges. Aunt Rene had heard what her mother said and when no one was around she took Sydney aside. She explained the importance of the work Sydney did. She made it clear that she was a wonderful scientist and encouraged her to try again the next year. Which she did and won.

There was a discreet knock on her door.

"Who is it?" Sydney wiped the tears from her cheeks.

"Syd, it's me." Mark's voice was level and soft.

"It's open." As soon as he appeared Sydney walked to him and placed her head on his shoulder. His arms felt like nothing she'd ever experienced before. Dependable, protective, trustworthy. Was this love?

"Are you ok? I heard your mother leave a few minutes ago." He whispered in her ear.

"I've been better." She heard herself laugh.

"Can I do something?"

Sydney reached up and took his face in her hands and kissed him. When she released her hands from his face, his hands took her face and he leaned in deepening the kiss. This was so easy, so right. It was time to tell him why she had walked away all those years ago. She led him into her room to sit on the bed together. She told him what her mother revealed. What she told her about her father, about Aunt Rene, about the relationship. She wanted him to know everything. No more covering up emotions. Life was too precious to hide from or to dwell on the past. They were here for the future, and for the first time, she'd do anything to ensure that future. She took both his hands and readied herself for what she was about to say.

"I need to explain why I left you in Boston." She stole a glance at his face.

"Boston? You mean when you went to work for the Institute?"

"Yes. I had gone to my doctor, um. . . my gynecologist that afternoon before our first year anniversary of meeting on the motor spinners. Do you remember that night? We went to a wonderful restaurant."

Mark nodded. He kept silent. She couldn't read his face so she looked away and plowed on still gripping his hands.

"They needed to run more tests to check unusual growths in my body." She felt his body stiffen.

"Cancer?"

"No! no, not cancer. But it was serious. The results came back days later. It was a condition that would be make it extremely dangerous for me to ever have children. I struggled with telling you and then my mother called the next day and offered me the job at the institute." Tears were streaming down her face but she didn't let go of his hands. "I couldn't do that to you. You wanted children more than anything else. I knew you would tell me that it didn't matter; that we could adopt or whatever. But I was devastated and so used to handling things on my own that I made the decision without even telling you. I'm sorry. I'm so very, very sorry." She realized that he had let go of her hand and moved his arm to embrace her shoulder bringing her closer.

"Syd, oh Syd. So many years wasted. I wanted you more than anything and if that meant no children I would've accepted it, as long as I had you." He took her in his arms and she broke into sobs as years of pain and loneliness poured out.

When she calmed down, she picked up her head and touched Mark's face. She found it wet with his own tears.

They stayed like that for an hour. Talking, holding each other.

"You know I'm here for you, whatever you need." Mark said.

Sydney could see the intensity in his face. He was here for her not just physically and emotionally. But, also, as a scientist. She felt the strength of his trust in her judgement, her expertise. She could see now that she had to move away from her mother's shadow and make her own success. Her own life. A life that would include the people she loved.

CHAPTER
FORTY-FOUR

••

h-ODD 12,930
Oxygen level 20.2

The next morning Sydney was up at six a.m. Last night she and Mark had discussed the next steps for the project and the situation with Art. He told her he wanted to follow up with the Puno police and the men from Katen's company. See if they had found any clues about Art's whereabouts. He made plans to meet with the police lieutenant and Katen's head security guy at Art's office by 8am. She figured she'd spend the few hours before the meeting going through the destroyed lab to see what was left of the equipment. As she stepped around the rubble of the lab site, she picked apart the details and next steps of their plan. The night before they had discussed several options. Both had come to the same conclusion. There was no time to investigate alternative methods or approaches to the oxygen depletion. They decided to continue moving forward with what was left of the original project. The development of new injections could be completed back in California. Afterall, they had the finalized blueprint DNA from the local people. While all the injections had been destroyed, the mapping of how to create those injections was safely stored in her computer. It was not necessary to stay here in La Rinconada. They would need to line up new test subjects, but she was sure that could be done in California. She shook her head as she continued stepping over the metal and glass debris. Some of the equipment survived the landslide and needed to be packed up. She made a mental note to talk to Dar.

The kink in the plan was her mother. Sydney was all too aware of her mother's determination to take complete control. She had witnessed that determination yesterday. And then there was Aunt Rene. She felt the need to clear things with her. Let her know that she knew of the relationship with her mother. Aunt Rene was a woman Sydney respected and admired, a woman with compassion and a strong, fierce intellect. Sydney had opened up to

Mark last night about everything. She knew clearing the air was the best thing for everyone. Proof in that she felt free of all that emotional baggage; she had never slept better. She smiled remembering his words about her mother and Aunt Rene.

"Just because Dr. Davis is your biological mother doesn't mean you are destined to be like her. You had Rene in your life for so long during those critical years. Environment is just as strong as genes. Even I know that." He laughed. "Genes aren't the whole story."

How right Mark was. She made her way along the road heading over to the security office. It was almost eight.

"Good morning, Sydney."

Sydney looked in the direction of the voice. Aunt Rene was walking toward her. "Dr... um. . .Aunt. . . um. . .Good morning." Sydney felt nervous. She suddenly remembered when they had last seen each other back in California. Aunt Rene had consulted at the Institute about four years ago. They'd barely had time then to exchange pleasantries. Sydney felt like her life was one missed opportunity after another.

Rene slowed her step and approached Sydney, "Please, it's Rene." She stopped when she was directly in front of Sydney. "I spoke with Ann last night, after she left your room. I'm so glad that she finally told you. I've been begging her to say something for so many years." Rene held her hands together as if she prayed. She then opened her arms.

Sydney wanted to go there. She could visualize it, yet she held back. What did this wonderful person see in her stiff cold mother? She looked into Rene's eyes and saw the woman she always knew as a child. And then she knew. Rene was a person who made you believe that there was good in the world. Her mother needed, no, it wasn't just a need – her mother could not live without someone who gave her this. And while her mother desperately craved this, Rene also needed Dr. Davis; a strong, bold woman. Fearless. They were a match.

Rene stumbled over her words, "I... loved you as a daughter, always loved you . . . and still do."

Sydney stepped forward into her embrace.

CHAPTER
FORTY-FIVE

h-ODD 15,670
Oxygen level 20.2

"We found the remains of Li Yun. His death has been confirmed." The agent from Katen wrote in his tablet as he spoke to Mark. Mark wanted to wait for Sydney, but the police lieutenant explained that they were rushed to complete the investigation. They were standing in front of Art's office. La Rinconada swarmed with new faces. The locals kept to themselves inside their small homes.

"Do you know for sure that it was Yun who set the explosion?" Mark asked the lieutenant. Mark had a hard time processing what was discovered about Yun. Being a member of a terrorist organization that recruited people to be environmental activists was one thing but planning and enacting such a violent deed was another.

"Yes, it was him. We'll need to talk to your son about what he remembered from the other night when he was in the mine with Li Yun and Art Saunders." The lieutenant was a short burly man in a uniform with mountaineering boots, khaki shorts, and a jacket. Mark wondered how he kept warm. The temperature hadn't gotten above freezing since they arrived. Mark stood shaking in his jeans, sweater, jacket, hat, and gloves.

"Yeah. I'll find a time you can speak with Ryan. But Art. Anything yet on his whereabouts?"

"Nothing yet. We believe he headed east toward Bolivia. Don't expect him to still be in the area." The man held out his hand to shake Mark's. "I've got to get back to Puno tomorrow and complete the processing for this incident. Please let me know when I can speak with your son." He turned and walked away.

Mark wound his way to Pa'qo's.

"Dad!"

"Ryan." Mark beamed when he saw Ryan running to him. Pa'qo emerged from the back room. "How's the shoulder today?"

"I rested well last night. My people helped me, and I took medicine. It was their time to cure me." Pa'qo gave him his iconic smile. "Ryan enjoyed playing with several of the children from the village."

"It's scary thinking about all this." Mark sat on the cushions near the window. "When Ryan told me what happened in the mine it was like some strange, weird story. But all the pieces do fit together. It's like Yun and Art were meant to meet."

"The men have not found the evil one yet." Pa'qo said this as a fact not a question.

"They said he left this area, possibly east into Bolivia."

Pa'qo crossed a hand over his chest and gently massaged the wound. "Perhaps."

CHAPTER
FORTY-SIX

h-ODD 16,100
Oxygen level 20.1

Sydney stood at the window of her room. She had lost track of time with Rene and had later been updated by Mark on what had been discussed during the meeting. Physically, her strength had returned from the ordeal with Art, but mentally she was finding it hard to concentrate on any one thing. The events over the past few days were unreal. Mostly she couldn't stop thinking about the deaths. Oxygen levels had reached an all-time low, 20.1. The numbers had piled up to over 16,000 around the globe. All asphyxiation or asphyxiation- related. And what happened to Art? The police said he was long gone. She felt her body being restored and wondered about Pa'qo natural remedies. The fact that his medicine worked shouldn't have been a surprise. She had studied alternative medicine and while some of the potions may have been unknown, it was something worthy of further study. She let out a slow breath and fell onto the hard chair in the room and leaned forward over her knees, her head in her hands. Darweshi and Mark were busy with the cleanup and packing of the lab. They were leaving tomorrow to head back.

Mother was standing firm on being the lead once they were in California. Sydney didn't have the mental strength to confront her here. Any delay, which a confrontation with her mother would certainly be, was something that could not happen right now. She must never lose sight of what they must do. They had time left. They had to have time left. But slowly that time was being eaten away, bit by bit. And all the while people were dying around the globe.

She glanced out the window and saw one of the locals walking to his home. These people were so resilient. Had so much inner strength. They had their beliefs that carried them through turmoil. And their leader was a spiritual man who believed in ancient remedies and that mother earth can heal. She on the other hand felt heavy and lost. Her insides ached, but not from physical pain. The thing inside of her, that unrelenting drive she always depended on, was disappearing. Someone shuffled their feet at the doorway. She took a moment to collect herself and looked over to the door.

"Sydney," his soft voice was unmistakable, "please don't worry." Ryan moved next to her and placed his hand on her shoulder.

"Oh Ryan." She pulled him into a hug. He didn't stiffen or push away. So different from even a few days ago. He had so much compassion for others. "You're such an amazing boy. I'm so lucky to know you." She released him and looked at his face, trying to read what was on his mind. "What is it, Ryan? Is there something you want to say to me?"

"I want to be with you." He remained still in front of her. "Are you going to keep working with Dad and the scientists here?"

She wondered if he could understand what the destruction of the lab really meant. If he could even fathom what was happening to the earth. Mark had told her that Ryan was intellectually able to handle the science of what they were doing in La Rinconada. He had explained everything to his son. But could he handle the psychological impact or the emotional tidal wave of this setback? She knew he deserved some explanation.

"I need to tell you something. The work we all came here to do has failed. I have failed. Your father did everything right. But the DNA injections were destroyed. We need to go back to California and start again." Ryan scrunched up his face and shook his head against her words.

She could sympathize with his denial.

"It is not a failure," Ryan shouted, "there is another way." He paused.

Sydney tried to calm him down. "I don't know what you mean, Ryan. Maybe you are confused. There is no other way."

He backed away shaking his head. His voice stayed tense. "I knew the CRISPR edit was not going to work. I know a better way to save the people. I tried telling Dad."

"Ryan. . . I'm sorry."

"No! I know. I have put it together." His face got red and his fists white. "The pieces fit. I studied about the potions and the medicines Pa'qo uses on his people. I understand now." Sydney sat silent. She wasn't sure what to say to him. Ryan was clearly struggling with something way over his head and she had no idea how to comfort him.

Then, he started telling a story. His eyes glazed over -- he was somewhere else.

"One night it was pouring rain. Mom had called Dad from her work. When they finished talking Dad came over to me and said that Mom was working late, and he brushed his hand across the top of my head. He laughed saying we were on our own for dinner that night. Then my brain started to burn." Ryan stopped and glanced over at Sydney. "That's what happens when my mind puts the pieces together, when I suddenly know what it all means." He stopped again. Sydney nodded her head for him to continue. "I remember grabbing Dad's leg and pulling on his pants. I told him that Mom brought her car to Eddie for new tires yesterday, but Eddie told her to come back next week. He didn't have time to do it right then at the shop. Dad didn't understand what I was saying to him."

As he talked the long-ago news article of the accident flashed into her consciousness. Sydney had followed Mark's career and had kept track. Two years ago, Catherine, while avoiding a client crossing that street, hydroplaned and jumped the guard rail into a ditch. She was pronounced dead at the scene.

Ryan's eyes were glassy. "I put together the patterns. Mom's bad tires, the people walking home at night on a street with no streetlights, the pouring rain. So many other things too. I knew it would happen." Sydney held out her hand to Ryan. He walked to her and laid his head against her shoulder. "I learned after that day to make sure people listened to me. I take it all in. Notice everything. It used to be a fun puzzle for me but after that night it was no longer a game."

She believed him. She had faith in this small exceptional child, that he had something she must listen to. "Okay, Ryan. Tell me. Tell me what you know."

"I need to show you." He grabbed her hand and yanked her off the chair.

Ryan headed outside and went toward an old overgrown mountain path. Sydney had never noticed this one. She felt confused about where they were going but allowed him to take the lead. Her mind was distracted by all that could be lost. They were so close to completing what they'd set out to do here. Even with all the tragic events, they were almost there. They would restart and finish this in California. She had discovered so much more than she could ever have expected. Ryan's voice broke her thoughts.

"I go with Pa'qo every day," he shouted as he let go of her hand and rushed forward along the side of the path as if all life depended on what he sought.

Sydney ran to keep up, staggering over the rocky surface. As the path got steep, Ryan slowed down and focused on a spot in the clouds above the glacier. His voice became gentler, "I am with him every day when he goes to heal his people. He gives them the plant. The one that grows in the ponds around the glacier. It is the plant that will save us." They climbed higher and higher up the path until he stopped short with his back toward her very close to the edge of the trail. She could feel the sweat on her body. Instinctively the fright of being so high and near a cliff edge kicked in. Ryan was still staring at the glacier.

She was afraid any quick movement might startle him. She knelt on one knee about three arm lengths away. "Come over here and tell me about the plant, so I can hear you better."

As Ryan turned, a man jumped from behind a rock and locked Ryan against the side of his waist.

"Sydney!" Ryan struggled in Art's grasp. Blood from the wound on his forearm stained Ryan's shirt. It started to bleed even more as he wrapped his arm across Ryan's throat.

Sydney stopped any movement the moment her eyes locked on Art. Ryan was too close to the edge. Her incapacitating phobia gripped her inside and shook her apart. As she stood, she could see the drop, almost feel it as the cold glacier air froze her in place. Ryan continued screaming her name.

"Shut up!" Art tightened his arm. "I've got no time for this bullshit." He yanked Ryan in front of him to face Sydney. "You need to help me. Fix up my arm and I'll let the kid go."

"Release him and I'll help you."

Art made a sound that was halfway between a laugh and a growl. "You think you're so smart. Come over here, now, or the boy goes over the cliff."

She took a deep breath struggling with her anxiety and cleared her thoughts of everything but saving Ryan. She slowly managed to put one foot in front of the another up the slope toward them. The gravel and ice beneath her feet were loose. If she thought too long about where she was, she would freeze again. One wrong step would send her mind into a crashing, dark place. She just about got there and reached out; Ryan responded by attempting to thrust his arms up toward Sydney. Art yanked back. Ryan's piercing cry echoed off the cliff and faded into space.

"Ryan!" Her arms reached into the empty space were they both once stood. Both were gone! A familiar dizziness overwhelmed her. Her balance gave way and she fell face first, landing on the edge of the cliff. She tasted the grit in her mouth.

Tears streamed down her face and mixed with the dirt. Her body embedded itself in a hole as if she was in a strait jacket of dirt and gravel. Every muscle in her body stilled absorbing all the fear that came from a dark place inside. Her mind convinced her to stay exactly where she was. "No. No! Not now!" She dug down deep, deeper than she had ever done before in all the meditations and sessions with her therapist. A desire bubbled through the panic and she shut her eyes tight concentrating all her thoughts on Ryan. She pushed herself to a seated position and lifted her head She managed to drag herself by her hands to look over the edge.

"Ryan! Ryan!"

She frantically searched over the edge. She immediately saw Art. He had landed on his side on a narrow ledge jutting out about ten feet from where she was. He was not moving but she saw his chest going up and down. He was still alive. She took a quick glimpse at the abyss below the ledge and clenched her teeth. Her eyes darted around, searching for Ryan.

"Sydney! Help me!" His shrill made her heart felt like it was banging against her chest. She ignored the bile rising in her throat and locked onto his position. His body straddled the trunk of a small bush and his fingers gripped at branches growing out from the rocks. He was to the side of the ledge where Art had landed. She could see the fear on his face as his legs dangled into nothing. The only thing for her to do was jump down to Art. She could reach Ryan from there, grab him, and pull him back to the safety of the ledge. After that, she wasn't sure. But she had to try.

"Ryan, I'm coming!" Standing up, she forced her mind to empty of everything but Ryan and propelled herself into the air over the cliff. It was like flying in slow motion. The air passed under her and seemed to cushion her descent. She landed and fell to her hands and knees, knocking the breath out of her lungs. When she recovered and established where she'd landed, she turned her head around and found herself staring at Art's legs. He was back on his feet looking down at her.

Neither of them had the chance to speak. The familiar sound of a low growl echoed off the glacier above them. Within seconds pounds of fur landed on Art's back. He turned in circles while screaming. His fist tried to pummel the animal but only hit air. The puma continued to hold on, her sharp claws digging into his flesh. Their fight became a deadly dance, each thrashing back and forth. Sydney scampered to the wall of the ledge and plastered herself. She couldn't tear her eyes away from the fight. The cat wouldn't release her grip and finally the weight of both tipped forward, careening them over the ledge. Her last image was of the cat's jaw widening as sharp yellow teeth made a ripping tear into flesh. She stood paralyzed. It was the large female, the one with the spot and the amber eyes. Art's scream forced her back to reality. Sydney focused on where Ryan had been when she jumped. His face was pale but still holding on to the dried bushes growing from the rocks. He appeared to be going into shock. She flattened on her belly in the dirt and straightened her arms as far as she could toward Ryan. "Ryan! Grab my hands." Her belly scraped against the rocks and her arms stretched so far that she was sure they would be yanked out from her shoulders. At last, their fingers touched and her hands found his.

Sydney tightened her grasp and pain streaked through her upper body as she pulled Ryan to her side. With him secured in her grasp she rolled to her back on the dirt. Ryan cried, pressing against her. Minutes later Mark screamed their names from the top of the cliff. Everything that happened next was a blur. She remembered holding so tightly to Ryan that her fingers turned white and numb. There were ropes and shouting and the feel of Marks' arms lifting Ryan away from her. She learned later that Darweshi had been on his way to talk to her about shipping lab equipment back to California when he saw her and Ryan walking up that deserted path. He had immediately found Mark and told him. Darweshi said he'd had a feeling something was not right. It amazed her how easily the influence of spiritual connections and the belief of other powers and energy resonated inside of her here, maybe inside all of them.

"Ryan was trying to show me something up there on the path." Sydney and Ryan were now safe and sitting again in Pa'qo's house. This was the third time she'd explained to Mark why they went on that path. He couldn't believe or understand what had made her take Ryan up there. She was exhausted. Along with Mark's inquisition she spent an hour with the police describing the incident. An officer from the Puno police force had found Art's battered and torn dead body at the bottom of the cliff. When she asked about the puma that saved her and Ryan, the officers shrugged. They found no evidence of the large cat at the scene.

"Yes, but why would you let him lead you up there?" Mark's voice was strained.

"It was my special plant medicine. I think Ryan believes it can help." Pa'qo interjected responding to Mark.

CHAPTER
FORTY-SEVEN

h-ODD 24,580
Oxygen level 20.0

"Quechua." Ryan said as he abruptly sat up in bed. Mark stood from his seat on the bed's corner and went to him. He had lost no time in examining Ryan carefully inch by inch after the incident and now continued to watch him. Sydney sat quietly on the chair near the bed bending forward toward Ryan as he spoke. She was anxious to learn what he wanted to show her on that path. What did he know?

"I understand it's the plant Pa'qo gave Sydney when she was sick, and it worked. But that was different from what we came here to do. The plant can't help people breathe more oxygen. Do you understand?" Mark attempted to be gentle and convincing.

"Yes, yes it can! The gene injection will not work!" His body shook. He pointed out the window toward the town. "The people took the medicine for many, many years. Pa'qo told me stories of others who came to live here from faraway lands. They wanted to make this place home. There was no OID, no way for them to stay alive here. It was the medicine. He said it is the miraculous power of Pachamama. But I know it is also about how quechua works inside of people."

Sydney shook her head. How could this be? How could Ryan know about the body and how it processes oxygen? Maybe there was something this plant adds to the actual chemistry in the blood. Her brain went into overdrive. She pounced on him like he was one of her scientists. "But Ryan how do you know? What facts led you to this conclusion? And explain to me why you say the gene injection will not work."

Ryan closed his eyes and turned his face to the wall. "Don't be angry with me." Sydney's heart went out to him. He was brilliant, a genius, but still so young with all the anxiety and uncertainty that goes with that. She could never forget this and admonished herself for not being more tactful with him just now.

Mark moved closer to Ryan. He brushed his son's curly hair back with his hand. "I understand all you have gone through. And you see so much more than we can. You have a gift,Ryan. Like your mom did. Will you help us? Can you explain to Sydney and me?"

Mark maintained the gentle touch. After several minutes, Ryan whispered. "Injections would help some. But it can't be used for everyone in the world." He still faced the wall.

Sydney looked on as Mark continued to ask questions. "Why, why can't the injections be used for the world?"

"It will stop people from being different. People need to be different. . .inside of them. In their blood and in their body."

Sydney came to the bedside, "Like biodiversity? Are you saying this injection would inhibit biodiversity?"

Ryan faced Sydney, "People will become extinct if you do the injection. The injection does too many changes inside making everyone the same."

"Holy shit!" Mark couldn't contain his reaction when the realization hit him like a steel wall. "He's right!"

"What?"

"Ryan is right. The genome is an ecosystem. Everything is in balance. This injection could change more than we planned. It could change the DNA of hundreds of other combinations making every human the same, reducing biodiversity, like you said. Reducing biodiversity will eventually lead to mass extinctions."

Sydney straightened her spine and gripped Mark's shoulder. "We have to stop this plan."

"We also need to understand how the plant that was used on you works. Ryan sees something in this plant that we need to unlock." Mark hit his com-chip. "I'm calling everyone to meet here. We need to work fast on this."

"Do you understand?" Ryan held his fists next to his body and looked at Sydney, "You remember my dad could not breathe because he did not have his OID?

Pa'qo gave him a drink of the water from the pond with the quechua."

"I'm listening. Listening to everything you say. Thank you, Ryan." She grabbed Ryan's hand soothing the tension there. She recalled how Mark had breathed easier after Pa'qo gave him the water. She had been so busy with the lab and CRISPR that she didn't take notice. . .but Ryan did.

Mark finished making the calls. Sydney glanced up. Ryan was in her arms and she had been whispering in his ear. She could feel Mark's surprise at seeing Ryan's tenderness toward her. Feelings flooded through her for Mark and Ryan. Ryan's genius may have given the world another chance, but it was the gentle soul inside the boy that saved her. She said to Mark, "We should have listened to him sooner."

"I know. I started things moving. I've told Darweshi to inform the new team, including Dr. Davis that there is a change in plans."

Sydney switched on her com-chip and activated the Institute's research library. She requested information on *microscopic bacteria impact on human chemistry*. In addition, she made a note to investigate nutrigenomics. The impact of nutrition on genes. Could there be some connection to this quechua plant and the stimulation of a gene that processes oxygen?

Less than fifteen minutes later everyone gathered at Pa'qo's. Dr. Davis remained silent during the proposal. Sydney informed the group that they would be gathering samples and analyzing the quechua plant here and developing a method for testing on humans using the test subjects that were originally slated for the injections. She proposed another group back in California would concentrate on the distribution and communication process.

When Sydney finished Dr. Davis flipped her hand back and forth dismissing the idea. "Another way? Impossible. There is no other way. I'll be back to the Institute in a few days where I'll recreate the gene edits from the blueprint. We've lost a few days, but I will save this from being a total disaster."

"No! Here is what will happen." Sydney directed her attention to Dr. DeSalvo. "You will work with Pa'qo to get a full breakdown of what's in the quechua plant." She turned and pointed a finger at her mother. "And you, Dr. Davis, need to get a full team of bio-scientists and chemists here. . .Now."

Dr. Davis drew back and the room quieted. She locked eyes with Sydney. Sydney didn't budge. Didn't blink. This was it. After a while Dr. Davis stiffly scanned the room. Everyone had moved closer to Sydney. Subtle but telling. Dr. Davis walked out without another word.

Sydney got right back on track. "Rene, I pulled up some cursory research on microbiota and conceivable changes in body chemistry. I'll send that information to you. And Mark you need to find out more of how this quechua plant works in terms of stimulating genes." She would deal with her mother later.

"Yes, yes. Nutrigenomics! Brilliant." Mark's head bobbed vigorously.

Rene had been watching the exchange and smiled, giving Sydney a slight nod.

"Certainly. The study of microscopic biome in the gut years ago yielded amazing foresight into the treatment of many diseases—diabetes and schizophrenia among them—and now, years later, we are studying its determinations of other changes in the body."

Sydney's voice reverberated in the small room. "Let's get started. We don't have a second to waste."

Mark stayed behind with Sydney as everyone else hurried to redirect the project at La Rinconada. In a matter of days, the mountaintop would be teaming with scientists and workers building a new lab. This lab would test the microscopic properties of the plants growing along the mountain paths and in the water.

Mark slowly approached Sydney and put his hands around her waist, drawing her to him. She leaned in and he stroked her back. "This is amazing. A discovery like this is your legacy. Using a plant, a natural way, instead of attempting to redesign humans – ingenious!"

Sydney shook her head, "It was your son, not me. Ryan did it. He watches everything and he learns. And, when he knows something's not right, he'll tell you in no uncertain terms." She smiled.

With that Ryan inched out from the corner in the room. She had forgotten he was there. Both Sydney and Mark stooped down as Ryan dashed forward and stopped short in front of them. Ryan grabbed both of their hands and forced them up, "Lots of work to do."

The morning before the team left, the clouds that had hovered over the glacier since they'd arrived became a semi-transparent gossamer and finally dissolved, revealing the immense blueness of the sky. The mountain of ice against the blazing sun played tricks with her eyes, sometimes disappearing completely and then returning like a giant jewel presented on a velvet cloth. Sydney thought of the knife. She never questioned Pa'qo. It didn't seem to matter anymore.

Their project high in the Andes had ended. Sydney stood on the front stoop of the boarding house blinking against the glare of the glacier and into the faces of the townspeople. Men, women, old and young, had gathered to hear her speak. Over the past several weeks this town had become her home. She would tell them that they had saved the world. That the plant here had been the solution – something her team would've never discovered if their original plan hadn't led them to La Rinconada. But could she say it was because of a plan? No. These people more than anyone else on earth knew it went beyond scientific explanations. The world would go on because of the inexplainable. Something she would've never admitted to a month ago. They would save the earth but not in the way they planned. There was a mystery here at the top of these mountains. A mystery that went back thousands of years, maybe even more. When she began to speak to the crowd, she saw him in the back with his colorful robes and felt hat. Sydney felt his energy merge with the energy of the people, of La Rinconada. There was magic here.

ACKNOWLEDGMENTS

As a debut novelist, I never imagined how many family members and friends would be tapped in the making of my book. As beta readers, amateur editors, and fact checkers, they helped in the gathering of information and made corrections that improved the story.

I acknowledge and thank every single person who contributed to my journey.

There are, however, three people who require special mention: Becky Butler, Nancy McMillan, and Barbara Occhino. Without Arts Escape, a non-profit organization for promoting creativity in adults founded and run by Becky Butler, I would never have thought this could be a possibility. Nancy McMillan, a writer and teacher guided me from beginning to end in the book's development. And Barbara Occhino, a marketing professional and entrepreneur, who inspired and pushed me to keep going.